CALL

Ruth looked at me sympathetically. "Listen, Tina," she said, "maybe you shouldn't go out with Dave. So what if his father's judging the pageant? I'm sure you could win without playing up to the judges. Just work on your talent and appearance."

"Hey, you're the one who was all for my flirting like crazy with him so he'd get his father to vote for me," I said.

Ruth shrugged. "I know," she said, "but I think I was wrong."

"Look," I said angrily, "you wanted me to win. Now *I* want to win."

"But you're using him," Ruth argued. "You're going out with Dave so he'll get his father to vote for you, so you'll get to be Miss Spring Valley, so Jeff will see that you're special, right? You're using Dave to get Jeff."

I glared at her, but I couldn't think of a response. Because she was right!

Call
Me Beautiful

Shannon Blair

BANTAM BOOKS
TORONTO • NEW YORK • LONDON • SYDNEY • AUCKLAND

RL 5, IL age 11 and up

CALL ME BEAUTIFUL
A Bantam Book / October 1984

For Randi

Chapter One

My mother is always telling me how lucky I am. And I guess she's right. I am pretty lucky— not just with big things, but with small things, too. Sometimes I worry about my luck running out—the beginning of school this year was one of those times. But Mom reassures me whenever I start griping about something, "Tina, you're a fortunate girl: you're healthy, you're smart, you're beautiful. You've got absolutely nothing to complain about."

And she's basically right. I *am* healthy. I hardly ever get colds. I've never been in the hospital, and I rarely see a doctor other than for a checkup. And then I think of other kids I know, like my best friend, Ruth, who has all these allergies and has to get shots every week.

As for being smart, Ruth's always telling me how she has to knock herself out just to get B's, while I get A's without even trying. She's not entirely accurate. I have to study to get A's, but not half as hard as Ruth does for her B's.

And though I think my mother exaggerates when she says I'm beautiful, in all honesty, I am sort of pretty. I've got a nice figure, and my complexion is clear. People are always telling me how gorgeous my hair is—shoulder length, brown, with lots of body—and how friendly my brown eyes are, especially when I smile.

I get along with my family, too, much better than most of my friends get along with theirs. Oh, my eleven-year-old sister Dorie and I have our occasional battles, but they're pretty mild. Like I'll yell at her to get out of the bathroom and give me a chance, and she'll tease me about fussing so much over a stupid date. I kid her that pretty soon she'll be fussing over dates herself. We have a pretty good relationship. My father is relaxed and easygoing, and he approves of almost everything I do. My mother's a down-to-earth, no-nonsense lady with a good sense of humor. My parents are happy together, and they're proud of Dorie and me. They rarely hassle either of us about anything. A lot of my friends' parents bug them about their boyfriends, but my parents, on the other hand, really like Jeff.

Jeff Drury's my boyfriend. We first met in freshman English at Spring Valley High, and we instantly began seeing a lot of each other. But even by the start of this year—our junior year—we had never officially decided not to date other people, even though neither of us had gone out with anyone else in ages. Sometimes I found myself wishing we *were* more clear-cut about our relationship: you're mine and I'm yours and that's it. Practically every girl I knew in the class had a serious relationship. But Jeff thought it was silly. He said it was possessive and led to jealous misunderstandings. He felt it didn't really mean anything for people our age to make such serious commitments. "After all," he said, "we'll both be going off to college and changing, and in a few years, we might not have the same interests." It was a realistic view—that's what Jeff believed—but I thought it was kind of depressing. Jeff was always planning for the future. Me, I'd rather think about the right now.

"He's a special boy," my mother says, "kind, sensible, and bright. Not to mention the fact that he's also one great-looking kid. You're a lucky girl, Tina." And I agree with her.

So there I was in the autumn of my junior year, Tina Steele, healthy, intelligent and pretty, vice-president of the junior class, captain of the cheerleading squad, popular at school, well loved at home, with a cute male companion. And on a sunny, brisk day in early November, my luck, it seemed, hit an all-time high. The Pep Club announced that I would be their candidate for Miss Spring Valley.

"This is so exciting!" Ruth squealed as we met at our neighboring lockers. She had gotten to school late and had missed homeroom period. "When did you find out?"

"During homeroom," I said. The previous week the different school clubs selected representatives for the pageant. Of course, not every club presented a nominee, but most did. That's how they do it every year, and then the tickets to the pageant are sold to raise money for charity. The vote was by secret ballot, so I had absolutely no idea anyone would vote for me.

"Well," said Ruth as we both fumbled around in our lockers, "in the past ten years, almost all of the Miss Spring Valleys were nominated by the Pep Club."

"So?" I was in the process of shifting books, sweaters, and two months' worth of accumulated debris in search of a library book.

"So?" The slam of her locker door served as an exclamation point. "You're sure to win. The Pep Club is the largest, most powerful group at school. Not to mention the fact that you're very pretty and popular. You can't lose."

I finally found the library book and closed my locker door. "What ycu seem to be forgetting, dear buddy of mine, is that the Pep Club doesn't get to choose the winner. There are judges, remember? Teachers and civic-leader types."

"True, but the Pep Club must have some influence," Ruth replied as we walked slowly down the hallway. "How else can you explain that it's had more Miss Spring Valleys than any other club?"

I struck a movie-star pose and batted my eyelashes flirtatiously. "Cause the Pep Club has such good taste in candidates."

I heard a long whistle from the other side of the hall. "Hey, Miss Spring Valley!"

I felt my face get red and grinned as Howard Evans, my bio partner from the year before, walked toward us. "Oh, come on, Howie, I'm just a candidate."

"Well, unless the judges are all wacko, you've got it made." And with a friendly wave, he moved on.

"See what I mean?" Ruth asked smugly as we ambled down the hall.

I stopped in front of my English classroom. "Listen, Ruth, let's not make a big deal out of this, OK? I mean, it's fun, and I'm flattered to be nominated, but let's not take it too seriously."

Ruth's pale, almost nonexistent eyebrows shot up and disappeared under her red bangs. "How can you not take it seriously? It's only the biggest event of the year."

Before I could think of a good response, the bell rang. "Yipes, I'll be late again," Ruth cried and dashed off. Looking back over her shoulder, she yelled, "Meet you after class."

Inside the classroom everyone was milling about and chatting while waiting for the final bell. I moved slowly toward my seat as kids congratulated me.

"Thanks, thanks a lot, gee, thanks," I repeated until I reached my seat. The girl in front of me turned around and grinned. Before she could even open her mouth, I found myself saying, "Thanks, Sharon," and we both started laughing.

"You're a candidate for Miss Spring Valley, aren't you?" Sharon and I both turned to look at the girl who had just sat across the aisle from me. "Yeah, Pep Club," I replied.

"Me, too," said the girl, smiling slightly. "Latin Club."

"Congratulations," I began, and suddenly I realized I didn't know her name.

"Helen. Helen Davis," she said. "Congratulations to you, too."

Just then the final bell rang, and the teacher began handing out quizzes. He gave us half an hour to take the test, but I finished mine in fifteen minutes. I glanced over at Helen Davis, who was going over her answers. She's one of those quiet sort of girls who always seem to be there, but you never really notice. I studied her face—not gorgeous, but interesting. She had large, dark eyes, a tiny nose, and nice skin. Her hair was pretty, dark and shiny, but she had it pulled up in a tight bun, which didn't do much for her. I couldn't tell much about her figure because she had on a baggy gray jumper. Well, Latin Club was composed of about ten hard-core intellectuals, none of whom were great beauties. Helen was probably the best-looking of the bunch, but not what I'd call tough competition. And suddenly I realized what I was thinking. I sat very still, shocked at my own thoughts. *Whoa, Tina, hold on there,* I said to myself silently. *You're the one who said you weren't going to take this business too seriously.*

It's all just for fun, remember? It's just a silly little beauty contest. Win or lose, it's not very important.

And I did really believe that. To be perfectly honest, I always thought those pageants were a little dippy. I mean, what's the point? Every year my sister and I watch Miss America on TV and crack jokes at the dumb talents and take guesses as to who will win. We have a system. A contestant gets plus points if she has a cute southern accent and minus points if she sounds like she's from New Jersey. If she sings opera or if she plays a piece on the piano that requires her to move her hands all the way up the keyboard, that's a plus. Actresses doing dramatic readings, ventriloquists, and baton twirlers, no way. Dorie and I get terribly silly and make all kinds of sarcastic comments about the competitors.

And now here I was, Tina Steele, a competitor myself!

Lost in my thoughts, I jumped when the guy behind me tapped me on the shoulder to pass his paper up to the front. The teacher began a lecture, and from then on I was too busy taking notes to think about the contest until the bell rang.

Chapter Two

I found Ruth out of breath outside my English classroom door. "I ran all the way from my class," she gasped. "They've posted a complete list of nominees."

Well, I *was* curious. They had announced all the candidates in homeroom, but I had been so excited when I had heard my name that I hadn't listened to half the others.

Ruth practically pasted her face against the sheet. She can't see much without her glasses, and she's too vain to wear them. Her parents refused to buy her any more contact lenses after she lost her third pair. "Let's see," she said, "Patsy McCoy, she's funny but not big competition. Laurie Rich, I'm surprised she even accepted the nomination. Donna Morelli, she's pretty cute. Uh-oh, Merrill Dellinger, her father's on the school board. Kay Thigpen, I can't believe it, she's got such a nasty personality."

I looked around to make sure no one was within earshot. "Keep your voice down," I whispered. "Oh, no—look who the Drama Club nominated."

"Vicki Gilligan! Now there's some heavy competition."

Vicki is in my history class. She's tall, with dark hair, and very sophisticated. She used to flirt with all the guys in the class, including Jeff—*my* Jeff.

I worried about that sometimes. Because Jeff and I had never made any kind of agreement *not* to go out with other people, I wondered sometimes if he ever thought about asking someone else out. Someone like Vicki.

Ruth was still contemplating the list. "Candy Robinson, too dumb. Marcia Jacobs, she's OK. "Well," she said, taking a deep breath, "I don't think you have too much to worry about except for Merrill Dellinger and Vicki Gilligan."

"What about Helen Davis?" I asked suddenly.

"Who? Oh, yeah, Latin Club. No sweat, she's probably terrible."

"Checking out the competition?" Jeff stood there looking faintly amused.

Ruth giggled and began explaining to him why I was sure to win. I just stood there, smiling and feeling the familiar rush of affection I always got when I looked at Jeff.

If I'd describe Jeff, he wouldn't sound spectacular. He's got brown hair and brown eyes, he's of medium height, with a medium build. But the way it's all put together is fantastic. He's smart and self-confident, and he always seems to understand what's going on. My mother says he's unusually mature for his age, and she's right. But there's something beyond all that that makes him special.

Ruth was still jabbering away. In midsentence she glanced at the clock, gave her standard shriek, and took off. Jeff and I began to walk down the hall toward our history class. "You don't really care about this Miss Spring Valley business, do you?" Jeff asked.

I grinned. "Of course not. It's Ruth who's making a big deal out of it." We walked along silently for a minute. Jeff had this funny frown on his face, and it was an expression I recognized. It's the way he looks whenever he's worried about something. "What's the matter?" I asked. "Don't you want me to be in the contest?"

We stopped outside the door of our classroom, and he looked at me seriously. "It doesn't matter what I want," he said. "I just hope you're not taking this too seriously."

I pretended to pout. "Don't you think I'm good enough to be Miss Spring Valley?"

Jeff didn't smile, but he took my hand, and a familiar tingle went right through me. "I think you're good enough to be anything you want to be. But I also think this beauty pageant stuff is silly and a waste of time."

For some reason I felt annoyed. "I know it's not important," I said. "I'm just doing it for fun."

Jeff nodded, but he still looked concerned. The bell rang and we went into the classroom. The teacher wasn't there yet, and everyone was moving around and talking. Jeff got into a conversation with some of the guys, and I made my way through another rush of congratulations. After about five minutes, Mr. Preston, the assistant principal, came into the room. "Mr. Spencer wasn't feeling well, so he's gone home," he announced. "I want you all to settle down and treat this as a study hall. We'll send the sub in as soon as she gets here." He tried to look threatening, but he wasn't very successful. Slowly the room became silent, and he nodded with satisfaction and left. Naturally, the second the door closed, we resumed our conversations.

"Weren't you excited?" Candy Robinson planted herself on the vacant desk in front of mine. "I went crazy when I found out this morning. I couldn't believe the football team would pick *me*." I smiled and nodded and let her prattle on. Trying to talk to Candy Robinson is very similar to talking to an empty house. She's sweet, but sometimes I get the feeling her brain is missing. "Not that I expect to win," she continued, "but it's just so thrilling to be nominated, don't you think?"

"I don't know that I'd call it thrilling," I replied carefully, "I mean it's nice, but it's not all that important."

Candy's pink and white baby face looked shocked. "Oh, but it is. I mean, Bobby's so proud of me. I bet Jeff's proud of you, too."

I glanced back at Jeff and noted—with some alarm—that he appeared to be in an intense conversation with Vicki Gilligan. "Oh, yeah, sure," I said and felt relieved when Bobby, Candy's boyfriend, came over and started talking to her.

I strolled casually over to where Jeff and Vicki were sitting. "Hi," I said.

Vicki turned and acknowledged me with a slow, lazy smile. "I was just telling Jeff that he should try out for the Drama Club's *Scenes*

13

from Shakespeare. Don't you think he'd make a wonderful Romeo?" I almost laughed out loud. Jeff was hardly an actor, and if he were, he'd be more likely to play a forty-year-old lawyer than a lovesick teenager.

Jeff spoke up quickly. "No, thanks, Vicki, I really don't think I'm the type. Besides, I'm going to be pretty tied up with the debate team this term. In fact," he said, turning to me with an apologetic expression, "you'd better not wait for me after school today. I've got a team meeting."

I knew Vicki was smirking behind my back. "How come? I thought the team met on Mondays."

"I don't know. I just got a note from the coach this morning in homeroom."

At this point Vicki broke in. "You know, there's not that much difference between actors and debaters. I mean, both depend on convincing an audience that what they're saying is true."

"You're right," Jeff agreed. "But there's a difference in what they're trying to accomplish." Jeff proceeded to explain some of the intricacies of debating techniques to Vicki. She had on this I'm-absolutely-fascinated expression, and I sat there feeling ignored and stupid. I tried to be polite and look interested, but I'd heard it all before. Actually I was very proud of Jeff. He was the best debater on the team. It did take a lot of his time, though.

"Honestly, Jeff," Vicki was saying, "I never realized how interesting debate could be. You know, I'm working on my audition speech for the Shakespeare scenes. Maybe you could give me some tips on making it sound more convincing." She punctuated this with an inviting half smile and a sexy, sidelong look. *Not too subtle*, I thought.

Jeff responded with a smile and a noncommittal shrug.

Vicki then turned to me. "Have you decided on a talent yet, Tina?"

I looked at her blankly. "Talent?"

"For Miss Spring Valley. There's a talent competition, remember?"

All of a sudden I got nervous. I'm talented, all right, but not at the kind of stuff that looks good on a stage in front of hundreds of people. Classwork and student government, yes. Shakespeare scenes or concert piano, no. I shrugged. "Actually, I haven't even thought about it. I mean, I'm not taking the contest all that seriously." I glanced at Jeff, and he smiled with approval.

"Well, I don't care about the title either," Vicki said, "but there's a separate award for talent, and I want to get into a good drama school when I graduate. A talent award would look awfully good on my application."

To my surprise, Jeff was nodding in agreement. "That makes sense. This whole beauty pageant thing is pretty superficial, but if you can use it to further your goals—"

The classroom door opened at that point, and a bored-looking teacher came in. Everybody stopped talking and moved back to their regular seats.

"Read chapter five," she announced flatly and sat at the front desk.

I turned around and looked back at Jeff. He winked. I smiled back at him, then opened my textbook. I couldn't concentrate on the chapter, though. I'm not the jealous type, really. I've never had any reason to be, and besides, I didn't think Jeff could be interested in someone as phony as Vicki. But there was something about that conversation that bothered me, and I couldn't figure out what exactly.

When I went over the conversation with Ruth on the way home from school, she didn't seem to think it was particularly significant. "Vicki's just another flirt," she said. "What are you so worried about? Jeff hasn't looked at another girl since the two of you started dating."

"But that's not what's bothering me. I don't

16

think he's interested in her in that way. It's just that, well, he seemed to *respect* her. He tells me the contest is superficial, but he thinks it's just great for Vicki."

Ruth shrugged. "So what? Jeff respects you. Doesn't he always ask you for advice when he goes shopping for clothes?"

"That's not the kind of respect I'm talking about," I snapped and immediately felt ashamed of myself. How could I expect Ruth to understand what I meant when I couldn't understand it myself? "Let's forget it," I said. "Come on home with me. We've got to come up with a talent."

Chapter Three

That evening at the dinner table, I told the family about my nomination. Dorie was thrilled. "Oh, wow, fantastic!" she said. "If you win, you'll get your picture in the newspaper, and maybe some movie producer will see it and make you a movie star!"

"For some reason, I doubt that many movie producers read the *Spring Valley Gazette* on a daily basis," Dad said. "But congratulations anyway, Tina. I always said good looks were a dominant characteristic of this family."

"Why, thank you," Mom said as she reached for another piece of my father's extraspecial fried chicken.

"I mean, great beauty tends to run in my family," Dad continued with a sly grin. "And, if our lovely daughters ever develop any culinary talents, I'll take the credit for that, too." He sighed in delight as he took the last bite of his chicken leg.

Mom reached over and punched him lightly on the arm. "And what, pray tell, do you think they have inherited from *my* family?"

Dad rubbed his shoulder in mock pain. "Well, if either becomes a first-rate boxing champ, we'll know who to thank for that."

"I was nominated by the Pep Club," I said, ignoring my parents' joking. "Did you know that in the past ten years, six Miss Spring Valleys were nominated by the Pep Club?"

Mom smiled, but her forehead wrinkled a little. "It's very flattering," she said, "and it's nice that your classmates think so much of you. But I hope there are other things that are important to you."

She was sounding just like Jeff. And again, I felt annoyed. "Of course there are. It's just for fun."

"I've never really understood the point of beauty contests," Dad mused, reaching for the last piece of chicken. "It's all so subjective. As some great person once said, 'beauty' "—and he raised a finger wisely—" 'is in the eyes of the beholder.' "

"Oh, very profound," Mom said teasingly. "And may I add that it's only skin deep."

"And," Dad continued, "fleeting."

"Hey, come on, you guys," Dorie interrupted, "quit giving her a hard time. I think it's great that Tina's going to be in the pageant."

I flashed a grateful smile at my sister. "Well, I'm glad somebody appreciates me around here," I announced as I got up to clear the table. "And besides, it's not just a beauty contest. There's a talent part, too, and they take other stuff into consideration, like grades and extracurricular activities. Plus, the money from the ticket sales goes to charity."

"But why is it always *Miss* Spring Valley?" Dad asked. "Why don't they ever give the guys a chance?"

"Tradition, I guess," I replied.

Mom sniffed. "A sexist tradition, if you ask me."

"Oh, *Mother*."

She came over to the sink, where I was running the water, and gave me a little hug. "Listen, sweetie, I'm not trying to put you down. I just don't want you to place too much importance on this contest." Before I could say anything, she continued. "And I know you won't. You're a solid, bright, sensible young lady."

21

I looked at her. She had this intense expression on her face, and I wondered if maybe she weren't taking the whole thing more seriously than I was. I gave her a reassuring smile. "Don't worry, Mom."

She responded with another hug and turned to leave Dorie and me to cope with the dishes. Looking back she added, "Maybe if you emphasize the grades and extracurricular activities, it might look good on your college applications."

"Hey, that's right," Dad said from the table, where he was looking at the newspaper. "Have you started sending away for college catalogs yet?"

"Not yet."

"Well, you've got time, but you should at least start thinking of some colleges you want to apply to," he said.

"I am, I am."

Actually, I hadn't really given it much thought at all. College seemed like a hundred years away. It wasn't, of course. Some of my friends were already sending away for catalogs and talking about where they were going to apply. I just couldn't get into it. To be perfectly honest, the thought of college scared me a little. You had to know just what you wanted to study. I enjoyed a lot of things and was good at most of them, but there wasn't one special thing I wanted to devote all my time to. Besides, I was having a great time in high school. Thinking about college meant making big decisions, planning for the future, all that depressing stuff. I just wanted high school to go on forever.

Jeff didn't. He couldn't wait to get on with his plans for the future. He knew just what he wanted to do. He'd go to a good Ivy League school and study political science, then go to law school, then work for the Legal Aid Society, and maybe go into politics. I know he'd be good at it, too. Whenever I hear him debate, I'm always impressed with how logical and convincing he is. He's got real talent.

Ruth and I had joked about what I could do for a talent for Miss Spring Valley—like maybe display all my report cards since first grade. I'd laughed about it with her, but actually I was a little worried. I can't sing or dance or play a musical instrument. I'm no good at reciting or telling jokes. So what was left? Arm wrestling?

I was still pondering this later that night when Jeff called. "Hi, Tina?" He sounded a little breathless, as if he were excited about something.

"Yeah, what's up?"

"This is really great. The Spring Valley De-

23

bate Team has been invited to a regional tournament in New York."

"Hey, that's terrific! When is it?"

"Early December. And it's a good topic, too, nuclear disarmament."

A pretty heavy subject, I thought. I wondered how much of his time it would take. "That sounds great," I said. "Is it going to be a lot of work?"

"You'd better believe it. All the top teams in the region will be there, and we don't have much time to prepare."

I could tell he was really thrilled about this, and I was honestly happy for him. "Oh, I know you'll do fine. By the way, the movie starts at eight tomorrow night, so—"

"Hold on," he interrupted. "I'm sorry, Tina, but I can't make it. I've got to meet with some of the team people for strategy planning."

"On Friday night? Can't that wait until Saturday?"

Jeff gave what sounded like an exasperated sigh. "I've got to spend Saturday in the library. Look, maybe we can get together after my meeting tomorrow night and get a hamburger or something."

I was beginning to feel a little irritated, but I

24

tried to keep my voice light. "OK, I suppose so. Listen, do you have any ideas for a talent?"

"A talent?"

"For the pageant?"

"What pageant?"

Now I was really feeling irritated. "Miss Spring Valley, dummy."

"Oh that. Don't worry, you'll think of something. Listen, Tina, I'll talk to you tomorrow, OK?"

What a great conversation. I got excited about his stupid debate tournament, and he couldn't even fake an interest in *my* contest. I was starting to get riled up when I realized how silly I was being. *Calm down*, I reprimanded myself sternly. *It's not a big deal. It's just a beauty contest, remember. Nothing to take seriously, right? Right. Absolutely and positively.*

Then why did I get this tingly feeling every time I thought about it?

Chapter Four

During the last period on the first Friday of every month, we have Student Council meetings. Student Council is made up of all the class officers, plus one delegate from each homeroom. I've been a class officer every year since I was a freshman. Some of the things we do are pretty important, like gather student evaluations of classes and choose the annual outstanding teacher. Occasionally we have a charity drive. But mostly we plan parties and dances.

On that Friday we spent most of the hour organizing the Thanksgiving canned-food collection for needy families. It shouldn't have taken too long. All we had to do was decide who would make the posters and who would collect the cans, but everyone was talking at once. It was all terribly disorganized, and Dave Powers, the Student Council president, just sat there, looking bored.

Dave ran for president last year when a shoulder injury forced him to give up football. Dave's the type who just *has* to be a big shot. I guess he figured that if he couldn't be captain of the football team, he'd be student body president. And he won the election because he's very popular.

I could understand why, although secretly I thought Dave was pompous and conceited. He *is* well dressed, though, and, to tell the truth, kind of sexy, with his athletic build and dark blond hair.

We finally finished with the canned foods, and Dave perked up. "OK, I guess that's all," he said and began gathering up the papers on his desk.

"Wait a minute," a girl called out. "We're supposed to get a report from the Miss Spring Valley committee."

"Oh, yeah, yeah, right," Dave said, his face looking interested for the first time during the meeting.

Lynn Pickens, the senior class president, got up. "There's not much to report yet. We're going to hold the pageant in the auditorium the

Wednesday night before Thanksgiving vacation. I'll send a notice to all the candidates telling them when they have to turn in a description of their talent so that we can make up the program."

"Is that all?" asked Dave.

"I think it would be appropriate at this time," Lynn added, "to acknowledge the two Student Council members who are candidates for the crown. Candy Robinson and Tina Steele."

Everyone applauded while Candy giggled furiously and I tried not to blush. I was looking straight ahead and noticed that Dave was staring at me as if he'd never seen me before. People started congratulating Candy and me, and I heard Dave say, "OK, that's all, meeting adjourned."

He was standing by the door when I got there. "Let's go get a soda," he said, and without waiting for a response, he put his arm lightly around my shoulders and led me out of the building. Dave has a tendency to think every girl in the world is dying to go out with him. And for a second, I wanted to pull away and say, "Not right now." But I was curious to find out why he was suddenly interested in me. Silently we walked across the street to a coffee shop where a lot of seniors hang out. I'm not sure why, but

I felt pretty cool walking in with him. Like I said, even though he's conceited, Dave Powers is a *major* big shot.

"So," Dave said as we slid into a booth, "you must be pretty excited about this pageant."

"Oh, I'm very flattered," I replied, "but I'm not taking it too seriously."

Dave stared at me. "How can you not take it too seriously? Don't you *want* to be Miss Spring Valley?"

I paused to think. "I don't know," I finally said. "I mean, is it really all that important?"

"Important! How can you even ask that? It only means—it means—" He seemed to be struggling for the appropriate expression. "Well, it means you're the best! Number one! Get it?"

I didn't know what to say.

"Look, Tina," he said. "I was Marcy Nolan's escort last year when she won. It was fantastic. There's this big drumroll, and then the announcer calls out your name. They hit you with this spotlight, and you walk out on the ramp all by yourself. Everyone cheers and applauds, and they play the school song. All the photographers take pictures, and the audience stands up. It's like a dream, like Miss America or something. Marcy was crying when she was crowned. Really, I swear, it could be the biggest moment of your life."

"It sounds wonderful," I said, and it did seem like fun but hardly the most important moment of my life.

Dave nodded with approval. "Well," he continued, "if you're going to win this thing, you're going to have to take it seriously. I mean, you've got everything going for you."

I managed a weak, "Really?"

"Sure! You're popular, you've got good grades, the teachers like you. You're obviously going to be one of the top contenders." He was talking just like Ruth, but there was something different about his tone. Ruth was excited about the pageant, but Dave really seemed to believe it was the most important thing around. He was very intense.

"Now," he said, "there are other candidates who are just as qualified as you are. So when you fill out the forms, you've got to shine, know what I mean? You've got to look just a little better than everyone else."

"I'm not sure I know how to do that," I said carefully. OK, I'll admit it, I was sort of fishing for a date. I had no intention of sitting home alone while Jeff caroused with the debate team.

"I could help you," he said. "Maybe we could

31

get together this weekend. How about tomorrow night?"

"Tomorrow night's fine," I replied. "Why don't you come over around eight, and we can go over the forms."

I left the coffee shop feeling sort of flattered. It had been a long time since any guy besides Jeff had paid attention to me. It wasn't that I liked Dave so much. For all his confidence and good looks, he was pretty shallow, especially compared to Jeff. I knew he was into status and his image and all that. Still, it was nice to be noticed, even though he wasn't the kind of guy I could get serious about. It was just the way I felt about Miss Spring Valley. It was an ego booster.

I didn't think about Dave again that evening. I was too busy waiting for Jeff to come by after his meeting and getting my weekend homework done. It was almost ten by the time he showed up, and he looked tired but incredibly happy. The minute he walked in, he started talking about the tournament.

"I think we've got a chance to win this thing," he said. "The whole team's really up for it. Tonight we divided up the subtopics, and if we can get all the research done in the next few weeks, we'll have time for practice meets."

"Do you want to get a hamburger or some-thing?" I asked.

"I'm not hungry. We sent out for pizza while we were working. But if you're hungry—"

"Oh, I'm not," I said, but I really would have liked to go out.

"Anyway, look, I've taken some notes on the areas I'm going to work on." And he proceeded to lecture me on details of nuclear disarmament. It was pretty interesting, but I was tired, and before too long an all-too-obvious yawn escaped.

Jeff wasn't offended. He even looked apologetic. "Hey, Tina, I'm sorry. I know I'm going on and on about this. I'm just so keyed up right now. I'll calm down. How about trying to make a movie tomorrow night since I had to back out tonight?"

"I can't," I said. "I've made other plans." In-stantly I regretted my coldness and tried to make up for it. "Really, I'm sorry, Jeff, but I thought you'd be working all weekend on this debate business."

"That's OK," he said cheerfully. Couldn't he have looked just a tiny bit disappointed? "I'm going to be working in the library Sunday afternoon, but I could take a break, and we could still make that movie."

"Maybe," I said. "Call me Sunday." I wasn't

going to let him think I'd just be sitting around waiting for him.

I walked him to the door, we kissed—somewhat less warmly than usual—and he left. This kind of thing had happened before. Jeff could get very excited about something when he was involved in it, something that had nothing to do with me, and then I always got a feeling I wasn't as important to him as he was to me.

At the same time I was feeling a little guilty. I suppose I could have shown more interest in his work, been more enthusiastic, whatever. But I brushed the guilt aside. After all I had important things on my mind, too. Like Miss Spring Valley. And I walked up the stairs to my bedroom, head high, my arms cradling a dozen invisible roses as the faint sound of a drumroll rang in my ears.

Chapter Five

Whenever I think of Saturday mornings in our house, I get this image of everyone running from room to room, bedroom to bathroom to kitchen, and out the door. Dorie's got piano lessons; Mom, who's a real estate broker, usually has an appointment to show a house; and Dad's got a standing tennis game. Conversation is minimal, mostly cries of "I can't find my shoes" and "Oh, no, look at the time." Once they're all out of the house—and leaving guess who with the breakfast dishes—everything's very quiet and I can enjoy my morning. Much as I get along with my family, it's nice having some time completely alone in the house.

Ruth knows our Saturday morning schedule, and she's got it timed to the minute. This particular Saturday no sooner had the last person slammed the back door when the phone rang.

Ruth didn't beat around the bush with the usual "Hello, how are you." "What's this I hear about you and *Dave Powers*?" she asked.

"Wow, news travels fast," I replied. "How did you hear?"

"I ran into Donna Morelli at the movies last night. And by the way, I've got some news for you, too. But first tell me, *what* were you doing with Dave?"

I laughed. "No big deal, really, he just asked me to have a soda after Student Council." Should I tell her he was coming over that night? *On the one hand,* I thought, *Ruth and I share everything. But on the other hand, she may be my best friend, but she does have a big mouth.*

"What does Jeff think about this?" she asked.

"He doesn't know yet. And besides, he's so tied up with the debate team right now, he probably wouldn't care."

"Dave Powers, hmmm. Well, I know he can act like the number one jerk-of-the-world, but he does have a lot of influence, and it wouldn't hurt."

"Wouldn't hurt what?" I asked.

"Your chances for Miss Spring Valley, of

course. His father is president of the Chamber of Commerce."

"So what?"

Ruth gave an exasperated moan. "The president of the Chamber of Commerce is always a judge, remember?"

"Oh, yeah, I guess." I groaned silently. Is this all we'd be talking about for the next month? "What's your news?" I asked, changing the subject.

"My news?"

"You said you ran into Donna Morelli and you had some news for me."

"Oh right, right. Like I said, I ran into Donna, and we got to talking about the pageant."

"What else?" I sighed.

"So I asked her what she was doing for a talent," Ruth continued, "and, get this, she's baking a quiche."

"Onstage?" I gasped. "That's crazy. A quiche takes forty minutes to bake, and we only get five minutes each."

"She's going to do it like that famous chef on TV," Ruth said. "She'll show how to mix the stuff and put it together, but she'll have a quiche already made that she'll present at the end."

"Gee, that's not a bad idea," I remarked. "I wish I had thought of it."

"You could make something else," Ruth said helpfully.

"No, Donna would kill me for stealing her idea."

"Too bad," Ruth said. "I'll bet the judges like that sort of housewifey stuff."

"I could demonstrate perfect floor sweeping," I suggested, and we both giggled at the image of me dancing around the stage with a broom and dustpan.

"How about mopping?" Ruth offered. "That's more work. Or dusting. You could get one of those pretty feather dusters. Or bed making. No, it would be too hard to get a bed on the stage."

"OK, OK, enough," I said. The joke was wearing thin, and I was getting nervous again thinking about my lack of talent. I was beginning to feel like a real loser, even though I knew that was completely untrue. "Have you heard what anyone else is doing?"

"Donna said Kay Thigpen is modeling clothes that she's making."

"I didn't know Kay made her own clothes."

"She doesn't," Ruth replied. "Her mother's teaching her to sew. I think it's just an excuse to show off her figure."

We were silent for a minute. "What am I going

38

to do, Ruth?" I asked finally. "I can't think of anything."

"We'll come up with something," Ruth said cheerfully. "What are you doing tonight? You could come over, and we could toss some ideas around."

"Can't," I said, and decided I might as well confess. "Dave Powers is coming over."

"Wow," Ruth said respectfully. "You *are* a fast worker. Getting Dave on your side might be even better than a fancy talent."

"Oh, come on," I said irritably. "I didn't ask Dave over to get him on my side, as you put it. Besides, this contest isn't that big a priority for me. I don't care if I win or not."

"What are you and Dave going to do?"

"He's just going to help me fill out the pageant forms."

"See!" Ruth said triumphantly. "You *do* care!"

I was beginning to get a headache. "Look, I've got to go," I said. "I'll talk to you later."

After I hung up the phone, I felt a little depressed. This whole Miss Spring Valley business was starting to get to me. I had thought it would be a lot of fun. Now it was turning into something I had to worry about. Maybe I shouldn't have accepted the nomination. Did I really need this aggravation?

And then I thought about Jeff. Maybe that's who I was doing it for. Because, despite the fact that he didn't seem very interested in the pageant, I had this feeling he'd be proud of me if I won. Or at least maybe he'd appreciate me more.

I sighed and tried to push these worrisome thoughts out of my mind. I decided to take advantage of the empty house to work up a new cheerleading routine I'd been thinking about.

I know a lot of people think cheerleading is silly, but, I have to say, I really get a lot of pleasure out of it. It's funny, though. Most of the girls on the squad love cheering and performing in front of the crowds at the football games, but they hate the practice sessions. I'm just the opposite. I don't mean I hate leading the cheers at games. That's fun, too. But what I really enjoy is all the planning and practicing. I like coming up with ideas for new cheers, original ones, cheers that aren't just "Rah, rah, go team, go." It's not easy. The words have to be short and straightforward so that everyone can understand the cheer with all the noise going on. And both the words and movements have to be simple enough to do at the same time. I don't want to put the squad down, but there are at least three girls who have a hard time remembering to say "fight" and kick their left legs simultaneously.

That time I was working on a cheer for when the team came out on the field. I struggled with it for a long time, finally coming up with something I thought was really good.

You better stop (pause), look (pause), listen
    and cheer,
'Cause the Spring Valley team is here.
We've got pep (pause), power (pause), spirit,
    too.
So come on, team, we're rooting for you!

I tried it out. The second line was out of sync. I inserted "football" between "Valley" and "team" and tried it again. Perfect.

Then I started working on the movement. I spent almost an hour trying out different patterns and at last came up with a combination I liked. I planned to teach it to the squad at our next practice.

I really enjoy going over the routines, breaking a cheer down into movement patterns, and working with the individual girls. Some, like I said, are a little clumsy, and I have to go over and over the same steps with them. I don't mind, though. I'm a pretty patient person. And

41

I get a big kick out of seeing it all pulled to-gether in the end.

I had just collapsed on the sofa when I heard the back door slam. "Lucky you," grumbled Dorie as she eyed me lying there. "I slave away at stupid piano lessons, and you get to lie around all morning."

"That's what you think," I replied. "It just so happens I spent all morning working up a new cheer."

"Oh, yeah?" Dorie said with interest. "Let's see."

Dorie might be a pain sometimes, but it's nice having a kid sister who looks up to you. Wearily I pulled myself off the sofa and went through the routine for her.

"Hey, that's neat! Teach me!"

"Later. I've got to wash my hair."

My mother walked in just then. "Going out tonight?" she asked as she plopped down into a chair.

"No, I invited someone over," I said and decided I didn't feel like going into details right then. "Had a rough morning?" I asked quickly.

Mom groaned. "I don't think that foolish woman has any intention of ever buying a new home. I'll bet I've shown her ten places in the past three months, and nothing's good enough for her."

"Who is she?"

"Mimi Powers. Honestly, the woman is so into status symbols. She doesn't even care how comfortable a house is; she just wants to make sure it's bigger and flashier than any of her friends' houses. Thank goodness her husband didn't come this morning. He's just like her, only worse. Don't they have a son at Spring Valley High?"

"Oh, yeah. Dave." I gave her a crooked grin and hesitantly added, "As a matter of fact, that's who's coming over tonight."

My mother looked immediately apologetic. "Oh, honey, I'm sorry. I didn't know he was a friend of yours."

"Well, I wouldn't actually call him a friend," I said carefully. "He's president of Student Council, and"—suddenly, I didn't want to tell her we'd be filling out the Miss Spring Valley forms—"we're working on some Student Council stuff." That wasn't really a lie. After all, the pageant *was* a Student Council project.

"That's nice," Mom said and rose to hang up her coat. An envelope fell out of her pocket. "Oh, I almost forgot. This came in the mail for you."

I took the envelope from her and opened it. It was a form letter from school.

Dear Junior:

We know you are all beginning to think about college. Choosing the right school to meet your needs, interests, and career plans is a big decision. Don't forget that we have counselors at Spring Valley High to help you explore all the possibilities. We offer catalogs, career option tests, and general guidance. Let us help find the college that's right for you!

I must have had a peculiar expression on my face as I read it because my mother was looking at me with concern. "Bad news?"

"Oh, no," I replied quickly, stuffing the letter in my back pocket. "Just a form letter from school." She still looked concerned, so I added, "From the counseling office. About choosing colleges."

"Might be a good idea to check it out," Mom said lightly.

"Yeah, right," I said. "I'd better go wash my hair." As I bounded up the stairs, I could almost feel her eyes still watching me with concern.

I wished everyone would stop bugging me about college. I mean, I wanted to go to college as much as anyone. But I had a lot of things to worry about right then. Jeff, Miss Spring Valley, and a talent for the pageant. Actually, that talent, or lack of one, made me even more nervous about college. Watching people like Jeff and Vicki Gilligan who were so sure of their goals made me realize how unsure I was myself. I had no idea what I wanted to study at college, so how was I supposed to decide which one to go to? I hated the thought of leaving Spring Valley. Here, I knew everybody, and everybody knew me. Here, I was *somebody*. When I went off to some strange, big university, I'd be nobody. I wished everything would just stay the way it was, Jeff and me together at Spring Valley High.

Why is it, I wondered as I stepped into the shower, *that some people know exactly what they want to do, while others haven't the slightest idea?* It was pretty depressing. I mean, you'd expect a mature, serious person like Jeff to know just what he wanted and what colleges would be best for him. Vicki Gilligan was a phony, but she thought she was the greatest thing ever to hit Spring Valley, so it figured she'd have strong goals. She was planning to become a big star. But even someone as disorganized as Ruth had plans. She wanted to attend the same ritzy girls' school her mother had attended. As Ruth cheerfully said, "It's a school for not-so-bright girls who can afford the tuition but can't get into the real prestige schools."

I was beginning to think there was something wrong with me. It was too upsetting, so I just pushed the whole question out of my mind and shampooed my hair. I wouldn't think about it that day. Later. When this Miss Spring Valley business was over.

46

Chapter Six

That evening as I was changing from my grungy jeans into some clean ones, Dorie burst into my room, without knocking as usual. "Could you knock?" I asked her sternly.

"Why?"

"Haven't you ever heard of privacy?"

"No." She flung herself on my bed. "I just had an idea."

"And I'm sure it's absolutely brilliant," I said sarcastically as I put on some lip gloss.

"Really, listen," she said. "It's about your talent for the pageant. Why don't you demonstrate some cheers?"

I grimaced. "Oh, Dorie, honestly. That's the kind of thing those no-talent types do in a teen pageant."

"You got something better?"

"No." I stared dismally at my reflection in the mirror.

"Well, think about it." Dorie hoisted herself up from the bed. "What time is Mr. Student Council coming over?"

"Eight. And do me a favor, would you?" I gave her my most plaintive expression. "Make yourself scarce, OK?"

"Don't worry about me," she said haughtily. "I'm spending the night at Karen's. What's the matter," she asked, giving me a mischievous grin, "you guys gonna get mushy?"

"Out!" I bellowed, and she ran laughing from the room. Just the idea of kissing someone other than Jeff made me ill. *So much for being able to date other people*, I thought. I wondered if Jeff felt the way I did about kissing other girls.

After I was dressed, I went downstairs and found mother sitting at the kitchen table making a mess out of painting her nails. I slipped the brush from her hand and took over the job.

"Thanks, Tina," she said. "I never could put on nail polish without painting my fingers."

"Where's Dad?" I asked.

"Getting dressed. We're going to the movies.

Are you and what's-his-name going to be OK tonight?"

"Mom!" I said. "It's no big deal. Like I said, we're just working on some Student Council stuff."

"On Saturday night?" she asked with a grin. "What's happening with you and Jeff?"

I sighed weakly. "Nothing, Mother. He's got something else to do, and I've got something else to do, and that's all there is to it."

"Good," she said, blowing on her nails. "Jeff's such a terrific boy."

Luckily Dad came in just then. I definitely didn't feel like talking about Jeff. "What are you going to see?" I asked.

My father made a face. "Some foreign thing your mother's insisting on."

Mom made a face back at him and said, "A little culture ain't gonna kill ya, kid."

They left, dropping Dorie off at her girlfriend's on the way.

I got the Miss Spring Valley forms together and sat in the living room to wait for Dave. Eight o'clock. Eight-fifteen. Eight-thirty. I had said eight o'clock, hadn't I? When it got to be almost quarter to nine, I was really annoyed. I mean, it's not that I was so anxious to see Dave, but there I was sitting around on a Saturday night and—the doorbell interrupted my thoughts.

He did look nice. I had to admit it. "Sorry I'm late," he said, "but you know how it is."

I didn't, but I let it go. "Sit down," I said. "Would you like a Coke or something?"

"Sure, why not," he replied.

I came back with Cokes and a bowl of pretzels. "I've got the forms right here," I said and reached to get them from the coffee table.

Dave put his hand on mine. "Hey, hold on a minute," he said. "I thought maybe we could just talk for a while."

"About what?" I asked stupidly.

"About us," he replied and punctuated that with a lazy grin.

I looked at him blankly. "What about us?"

Dave grinned again. "Well, like, I always see you with that Drury guy. You going out with him or what?"

"Jeff is a very close friend," I said carefully, "and we go out together a lot, but I wouldn't say we're 'going out' exactly."

"So maybe there's a little room for someone else in your life, huh?"

He really did come on like a jerk. But on the other hand, it wouldn't hurt if Jeff realized that someone else found me—interesting. So I smiled in a noncommittal sort of way and reached again for the forms. That time I made it.

"I've filled out the top part," I said. "It's just the usual stuff, grades and extracurricular activities."

"Let me see." He took the paper from me. "Didn't you do the introduction for last year's sophomore skit at the homecoming assembly?"

"Sure," I said, "but I wouldn't call that an extracurricular activity."

"I would," he said, and he penciled it in. "Look, Tina, if you're going to win this pageant, you've got to do everything you can to look better than the others." He made it sound so underhanded. "OK, here's the big question," he continued. "What would being Miss Spring Valley mean to you?" I didn't say anything. "So," he said, "what *does* Miss Spring Valley mean to you?"

I shrugged. "I don't know. I guess it would be fun—"

Dave gave me a withering look. "That won't get you any points. How about—" He paused to think. It must have been a colossal effort. "How about, 'Miss Spring Valley would mean that I was a representative of our school and its ideals, that I would be setting an example for the youth in our community.'"

"Oh, come on," I said and groaned. "That

sounds like one of those dumb contestants on TV."

"They're the ones who win," he remarked, and again he made a note on the form.

Well, that's how the evening went. I wanted to put down simple, short answers, basically just a list of things I'd done. But for every question, Dave wrote in some phony, grandiose statement that made me feel like a politician on the campaign trail. I began to feel like a product he was writing commercials for. Luckily my parents came home around ten-thirty.

After introductions Mom made some coffee, and we all sat around. Dave looked uncomfortable.

"I understand you're a senior, Dave," Dad said.

"Uh, yeah." I should have figured he'd be the type who couldn't carry on a conversation with adults.

"What are your plans for next year?" Mom asked.

"Uh, I'm going to Spring Valley Community College."

I was surprised. "I thought you were going to the state university."

"Yeah, I was supposed to," Dave said, "but then I found out that freshman couldn't have cars on campus. I'm getting this fantastic little foreign number for graduation, and I sure don't want to leave it here." With that he got up and said, "I'd better get going."

My parents said goodbye, and I walked him out the door.

"Thanks for the help," I said.

He leaned forward a little as if he wanted to kiss me, so I took a step backward. He gave me his famous grin. "I'll be calling you," he said and walked away.

I giggled to myself. *Was that a promise or a threat?* Then I went back into the house.

"Won't go away to college because he can't bear to leave his car," my father muttered, and shaking his head in bewilderment, he wished us good night.

"Well," Mom said brightly, "he seems—nice."

"Sure," I said, "just like his mother." And we both laughed.

Chapter Seven

There's nothing like lying in bed on a Sunday morning. On that particular Sunday I woke up around nine, but then I just lay there for another hour thinking about Jeff. Being with Dave the night before had made me even more sure of just how wonderful Jeff was. I thought about the two of them. If I had to be objective, I'd say Dave was probably better looking—in a plastic way, like the guys in magazines advertising blue jeans. But Jeff had it all over Dave when it came to personality. It wasn't just that Jeff was nicer. He was more intelligent, more down-to-earth, more sincere. . . . As I was piling up the adjectives, I could hear the phone ringing in the hall, then came a light tap on my door.

"Tina, it's Jeff on the phone."

Hey, maybe I have ESP! I thought as I bounced out of bed, threw on my robe, and dashed from the room.

"Hi, sweet." He calls me that sometimes. "Sweet." For a serious guy, Jeff can be very romantic. That's something else that's special about him.

"Hi, how's it going?"

"OK. I missed you last night."

I was silent for a minute, remembering the dull evening with Dave and thinking how much nicer the evening would have been with Jeff. "I missed you, too," I said. "How's the debate coming along?"

He sighed, and I could tell he had been working a lot. "It's hard, Tina," he said. "I guess I'd never realized what a complicated issue this is."

I felt sympathetic and a little embarrassed. Here I'd spent an evening fussing over a silly thing like a high-school beauty contest, and he'd been struggling with the pros and cons of nuclear disarmament.

"What side is the Spring Valley team arguing?" In debating you don't necessarily take the side you agree with, so you might end up making a case for something you hate. That's because debating isn't mainly concerned with the issue at hand but with the techniques of a good, logical argument.

"We're taking the pro-disarmament side, and I'm glad about that. But it's an emotional issue, and it's not easy uncovering the facts."

My sympathy level rose. "And you were probably up all night worrying about it."

"Not really," he said. "I worked with a couple of the guys until about seven, and then we went out to Gino's for pizza. We ran into some kids from school there, so we ended up staying until about ten."

"Who was there?"

"Betsy James, Howie Evans, Leslie Stern, and Vicki Gilligan."

My sympathy level went down. *Way* down. "How's Vicki?" I asked carefully.

Jeff laughed. "She's really something, you know? She'd been practicing her speech for the Shakespeare auditions, and she got right up on a table at Gino's and delivered it."

Show-off, I thought, but I forced a chuckle. "How'd she do?" I shouldn't have asked. I had a feeling I didn't want to know Jeff's answer.

"Excellent." I was right. "She's very talented," he continued. I felt sick. "But a little fake," he added. I felt better.

"Are you going to the library today?" I asked.

"Just for an hour. Why don't you meet me there about one-thirty, and we'll go to the two o'clock movie?"

"Great, I'll be there."

I floated back to my room to get dressed. I was fumbling through my sweaters when Dorie burst in, fresh from her overnight visit. "Did you figure out a talent last night?"

"No," I said, my voice muffled by the sweater I was pulling over my head.

"Well, you'd better come up with something fast," she said. "There's not that much time until the pageant."

"For crying out loud, Dorie," I snapped, "you act like it's the most significant event in the world! You know, there are more important things to think about!"

"Like what?"

"Like—like nuclear disarmament!" I sputtered, and I marched out of the room.

Dad always fixes a big breakfast on Sunday. That day it was cheese omelets, bacon, fried potatoes, the works. I was ravenous.

"Good morning," I said.

Dad stopped beating eggs for a minute to present a cheek for a kiss.

"Good morning, daughter number one," he

replied. "Do you want your omelet with or without onions?"

"With. No, wait," I said, remembering my date with Jeff. "Without."

Mom looked up from the newspaper and smiled. "May I conclude from that decision that you are seeing Jeff today?"

"You got it," I said happily and reached for the toast.

"Anything exciting in the news?" Dad asked. Mom glanced back at the front page.

"Well, everything's going up," she said, "interest rates, housing, college tuition—"

"Tell me something new," Dad said. "I'll need to be a millionaire by the time Dorie's ready for college."

"Don't worry, Daddy," Dorie said soothingly. "I'm going to start buying state lottery tickets every week so that I'm sure to win by the time I'm eighteen. You won't have anything to worry about."

"Whew, what a relief," Dad replied. "Thank you, dear."

"You know, I was thinking about that," I said carefully. "College costs and all. I mean, it's not just tuition. It's the dorms and food and travel. That gets awfully expensive." Dad nodded. "So I was thinking," I continued, "I mean, maybe, you know, I should take a job for a year or so, save my money, and go to college a year later."

Frowning, Mom looked up from her paper. My parents shook their heads simultaneously. "There's no need for that," Dad said. "Your mother and I have put aside money in a special account for both of you girls. I'm not saying it's going to be easy, but the money is there for you both to go to good schools."

"I don't understand why you're so worried about college, Tina," Mom said. "You've always done so well at school."

"I'm not worried," I lied. "It's just that—well, things will be different."

"But that's what makes life exciting," Mom said.

I just nodded and decided to change the subject. "I've got to come up with a talent for the Miss Spring Valley pageant. Any suggestions?"

"I saw a movie about a beauty pageant where a girl showed how to pack a suitcase," Dorie said helpfully.

"Thanks a lot," I said, giving her a withering look.

"You've got lots of talent," Dad said firmly. "Just think of a way to show it off." Big help.

*　　*　　*

It was an absolutely gorgeous, crisp autumn day, and the public library was practically empty. I found Jeff and his debate team buddies in the back at a large table, which was piled high with fat books and stacks of index cards. The entire group looked up as I approached, and they greeted me with smiles and mumbled hi's.

"I called the theater," Jeff whispered, "and the movie doesn't start until three. I'd like to work for another hour if you don't mind."

"Sure, that's OK," I said. "I'll browse a little."

"Great." He gave me a big smile. I mentally patted myself on the back for being so understanding.

I made my way toward the corner where the young adult paperback books were kept on a special rack. As I passed through fine arts, I spotted a familiar face. It was the girl from my English class, the Latin Club candidate for Miss Spring Valley. What was her name? Helen something.

"Hi, Helen," I whispered.

She looked up from the oversize volume that she had on her lap. "Tina, hello," she said, smiling pleasantly. By then I was close enough to see what she was reading. It was a music score, I could tell that much, though how she could read those symbols was beyond me.

"What are you doing?" I asked.

"Trying to pick out a piece for the pageant."

"What do you play?"

"Violin."

"Wow." I was impressed. The violin was such a beautiful instrument, and I knew it was hard to master. "How long have you been playing?"

"Since I was five. My parents say I used to hum along with their classical music records. They thought I might have an ear for it, and so they started me with lessons."

"Do you like playing the violin?"

She smiled, and her eyes lit up with a glow. She looked pretty when she smiled. "I love it. I guess it's probably the most important thing in the world to me. When I play the violin, I feel like I'm in another world, sort of like I'm floating on clouds, making the universe sing—" She stopped suddenly and blushed. "I guess that sounds pretty crazy."

"No, not at all," I said. "I think you're lucky to have something you care about so much. Do you plan to become a professional musician?"

She nodded passionately. "That's what I want more than anything. I'm hoping to get into a major music school when I graduate, and some day play in a symphony orchestra."

Another person who knows exactly what she wants to do with her life, I thought. "Do you have to practice a lot?"

"Every day. That's why I'm not involved in school activities much. I either have a lesson right after school, or I have to go home to practice. I know I'm probably missing out on things."

"You're not missing much," I said. "What you're doing seems a lot more important."

She looked surprised. "You think so? You're so active at school, Student Council, cheer-leading, all that."

"How did you know I'm a cheerleader if you're not involved in school activities?"

She smiled slightly. "You're pretty well known at Spring Valley High, even to people like me who don't get around much." I didn't know what to respond to that. "Besides," she continued, "I go to football games occasionally. My kid brother's in the marching band."

We were silent for a moment. "How do you feel about the pageant?" I suddenly asked.

She shrugged. "It's all a little shallow, isn't it? I thought it might be a way to get to know people better."

"Is that what you're going to play?" I asked, indicating the music score she was holding.

"I haven't decided yet." She reluctantly closed the book and placed it back on the shelf. "Actually, that's not what I'm supposed to be doing. I'm trying to do my calculus homework, but I'm having an awful time with it."

Now calculus is one of my favorite subjects. I like geometry, too, and trig. I love the way math is so neat and logical. When I'm working on a problem, I feel like I'm attacking a giant puzzle, and I get a real sense of accomplishment when I figure it out."

"Which calculus class are you in?"

"Beginning," she said. "What about you?"

"Advanced," I said and tried not to sound as if I were boasting.

"Wow," she said respectfully, and then hesitantly she asked, "Do you have a minute? Maybe you could explain something to me. I'm really dumb when it comes to math."

"Sure," I said. It was as good a way as any to kill the hour, so I sat down at the table next to her.

"I can't figure this one out," she said.

I took a look at the problem. It was pretty basic. "Oh, that's not so rough," I said reassuringly. "Here, watch." And I wrote a formula down on paper. Then I broke the problem down into parts and showed her how to fit the parts into the formula.

"You're good," she said. "Gosh, I think I almost understand it! You explain it so much better than my teacher. It actually makes sense!"

Her words sent a warm rush through me. "I'm glad," I said. "Are there any other problems you're having trouble with?"

"All of them," she said with an exaggerated gesture, and we both laughed.

"Well, let's get to work," I said. We went through each problem, and the hour flew by. Before I knew it, Jeff was standing by us.

"Hi. Jeff, do you know Helen—?" I stopped suddenly because I couldn't remember her last name.

"Davis," she finished. "Hi, Jeff."

"What have you two been doing?"

"Tina just saved me from flunking calculus." Helen laughed and gave me a grateful look. "She's a terrific teacher."

Jeff grinned. "She's terrific all right." I just basked happily in the glow of all that appreciation. "We'd better get going," Jeff said, "or we're going to miss that movie."

"What movie are you going to see?" Helen asked.

"*The Werewolf Meets Dracula's Daughter*," I said, embarrassed. She'd probably think it was a dumb movie to see.

"Oh, it's great," she said. "I took my brother last week." I must have looked surprised because she added, "I love old horror movies."

"Who wins?" Jeff asked. "The werewolf or Dracula's daughter?"

"Neither," Helen replied, laughing. "They fall in love, get married, and have little hairy, bloodsucking babies." We all started laughing, and I got up to leave. "I can't thank you enough, Tina," Helen said.

"Glad to help you anytime," I said. "We should get together soon." I meant that, too. I wasn't just being polite. I really wanted to get to know her better.

"I'd like that," she said, and we both smiled.

"She seems nice," Jeff said as we walked down the street toward the movie theater.

"She is," I said. "She's in the Miss Spring Valley pageant, too."

"Really? She doesn't seem like the type."

I stopped. "Why?"

"I don't know. I guess because she always looks so serious."

"And being in the pageant is something only an airhead would do?" I asked, my voice rising. "Someone like me?"

Jeff gave me a quizzical look. "Hey, come on, Tina, that's not what I meant, and you know it."

I knew that wasn't what he'd meant, but still I felt defensive. I just stood there, staring at him.

Suddenly he took my hand and squeezed it. "Hey," he said, "as far as I'm concerned, sweet, you *are* Miss Spring Valley. Also Miss America, Miss Universe, Miss—Miss Galaxy."

I looked up at him. His face looked serious, sincere, and loving. I returned the squeeze. "OK, Mr. Galaxy," I said. "Let's go meet the werewolf."

Chapter Eight

I think the movie was supposed to be scary, but instead, it was hysterically funny. We ran into some kids from school, and we all sat together. Sometimes we couldn't even hear the sound because we were all laughing so hard. Like when Dracula's daughter bit someone's neck and the blood ran down her chin. It was supposed to be gruesome, but the color was so bad that the "blood" was purple, and it looked like she was slurping grape juice. You could always tell when something exciting was about to happen. Two teenagers were kissing in a car, for instance, and some eerie music began to play. Then the girl glanced into the rearview mirror and let out a piercing scream. Of course, a hairy werewolf had appeared behind the car.

During scenes like this, I'd pretend to be startled and grab Jeff's hand. Then we'd both look at each other and crack up laughing.

Afterward a group of us stood outside the theater and started laughing all over again as we went over some of the movie's more ridiculous moments. Howie Evans went into a werewolf routine and pretended to attack Merrill Dellinger. Merrill made some crack about Howie needing a shave.

"Gee, I don't know about the rest of you guys, but I thought it was scary," said Candy Robinson, clutching Bobby's arm. Everyone groaned in unison.

"Oh, come on, Candy, you weren't really frightened by those dumb monsters, were you?" I asked.

She nodded vigorously. "If Bobby hadn't been sitting next to me, I'd have jumped out of my seat." She looked up at him with adoring eyes, and he beamed at her. *Is that what guys like?* I wondered. *Girls who behave like helpless babies?* I looked at Jeff. He was watching Candy with an amused expression. I caught his eye, and he winked.

The sun was setting as we strolled back to my house. I was feeling a little chilly, and I must have shivered because Jeff put his arm around my shoulders. It was lovely and romantic, and I felt I'd be perfectly content just to walk like that for hours without saying a word. Jeff broke the silence.

"Tina, I know I've been spending a lot of time away from you the past two days. And I know it must seem like I'm ignoring you." He was right, but I didn't say anything. He went on. "I just want you to know that you're still very special to me. I mean, you're the only girl in my life. You know that, don't you?"

"I know, Jeff," I said softly, and I put my arm around his waist. We walked along silently for a few minutes. I knew there was something else he wanted to say. Finally he cleared his throat.

"The thing is, I'm going to be pretty busy for the next few weeks. There's still so much research I have to do, plus practice meets. . . ." His voice trailed off, and he gave me a sidelong look. I think he was trying to see if I was getting angry, but I kept my face expressionless. "So," he finished, somewhat hesitantly, "I may not be able to see you as much as I'd like to."

I can't say I was thrilled to hear this. The whole debate-team business was beginning to get on my nerves, and it bothered me to think I wouldn't be seeing Jeff regularly. But I was trying

71

to be mature and understanding. "That's OK, Jeff," I said lightly. "I know how important this tournament is to you. But you won't forget about the football game Friday night, will you?"

"Of course not," he said reassuringly. "And isn't there something going on afterward?"

"Patsy McCoy's having a victory party at her house."

"Great," he said and then added teasingly. "You're that sure we'll beat Franklin Park?"

"Of course we'll win," I stated with mock indignation. "Have a little faith in your own school."

"OK," he said, grinning. "After all, how could the team lose when the most beautiful girl in the world is cheering them on."

"Speaking of cheerleading," I said, "Dorie thinks that's what I should do for my talent in the pageant."

Jeff's forehead wrinkled. "Oh, you can think of something better than that. I mean, you're a terrific cheerleader," he added hastily, "but you're good at so many things."

"Like what?"

"Well," he said thoughtfully, "like calculus. Everyone knows you're an incredible math whiz."

"Great," I said sarcastically. "I can really produce a terrific talent routine out of that. What am I going to do? Draw a huge equation on a blackboard and work it out? I'm sure I'd get a standing ovation for *that*."

"It's not a very flashy talent," Jeff admitted, "but don't sell yourself short. I mean, Candy Robinson sure couldn't do that."

"I wonder what Candy will do?" I mused. "Demonstrate how to put on eye makeup?"

"Maybe a speech on the meaning and significance of lip gloss," Jeff contributed.

I sighed. "I know it's dumb, Jeff, but honestly, cheerleading is the only flashy thing I can do."

Jeff gave my shoulder a squeeze. "Well, whatever you do, sweet, you'll be terrific." The way he said it, I could almost believe it.

"Can you stay for dinner tonight?" I asked. My father always makes something fancy for Sunday dinner.

Jeff's eyes lit up. "Hey, that's right, it's Sunday! What's your father cooking up tonight?"

I punched his arm lightly. "Do I have to tell you the menu before you decide?"

He pretended to look as if he were in the throes of serious decision-making.

"It's like this, sweet," he said. "You know I'm crazy about you and your family, but if it's liver and onions—"

73

I glared at him. "How dare you suggest that my father would even consider liver and onions?"

Jeff looked thoughtful. "Well, after all, there was the time he made that stuffed cabbage." I had to admit the stuffed cabbage had not been among my father's most successful experiments.

"OK, OK," I said, laughing. "I'll give you a hint. What has beef and noodles and sour cream and—"

"Stroganoff!" he yelled in delight.

"May I assume that means you're staying?"

But we were doomed to disappointment. There was no telltale stroganoff aroma as we entered my house, and my mother and sister greeted us with mournful expressions.

"Your father got a call from the office and had to go out of town for a meeting tomorrow morning," my mother said in a despairing tone. "I don't know what we're going to do about dinner." We all sat around glumly for a few minutes. Mom finally pulled herself off the sofa. "OK, kids, what do you want on your pizza?"

Dorie gave a whoop. She likes pizza much better than stroganoff.

I must say, the sight of that hot pizza smothered in pepperoni was a cheerful one. We sat around the kitchen table and stuffed ourselves. Jeff and I entertained Dorie and Mom with a rehash of the movie. It was so nice sitting in our cozy kitchen, laughing and acting silly, that it seemed as if all my problems about college, Miss Spring Valley, Jeff and the debate team, were dissolving away.

Then the phone rang, and Dorie jumped to get it. She was back in an instant. "Tina, it's for you," she said and then started giggling. "I think it's Dave Powers." I gave her a scathing look and went to the phone.

"Hello?"

"Hey, Miss Spring Valley."

I glanced nervously toward the kitchen and lowered my voice. "Hi, Dave. Listen, can I call you back? We're in the middle of dinner."

"Sure, babe. Just don't wait too long. There's a show on TV I want to see, and I hate to be interrupted."

I jotted down his number and went back into the kitchen trying not to look guilty.

But Jeff didn't even seem curious. He was in the process of describing the debate team's strategy for the tournament. "And so we're going to avoid the usual scare tactics and concentrate on facts and figures." Mom was nodding and asking him questions. I only half listened to their conversation because I was too busy wondering what Jeff would say if he knew Dave

Powers was interested in me. I got my answer a few minutes later.

"Come on, Dorie," Mom said. "Let's clean this place up and give Jeff and Tina some time alone." I shot her a grateful look, and Jeff and I went into the living room.

"What's Student Council been up to lately?" Jeff asked suddenly.

Ah-ha! He is curious, I thought triumphantly. "Not much," I said nonchalantly. "The usual. Canned goods collection for Thanksgiving. Miss Spring Valley, of course."

Jeff began poking through the record collection under the stereo. "It's amazing you guys get anything accomplished," he murmured, "with that jerk Powers as president."

I felt a little thrill. *He's jealous!* All of a sudden I felt an evil urge to let him stew a little. "Oh, he's not so bad," I said casually. "A lot of the kids think he has style." I didn't say what kind of style.

Jeff gave a grunt. "I suppose you could call arrogance a style. Personally, I never could figure out why that guy thinks so highly of himself."

"I don't know," I said. "But he *is* good-looking. And a pretty good athlete. And—" I hesitated a second. Should I? Why not? "And he's helpful," I finished.

Jeff looked up from the album cover he was reading. "How do you mean helpful?"

OK, I thought, *here goes*. "He dropped by the other night to help me fill out my Miss Spring Valley forms."

There was silence. "Did he ask you out?"

"Not really."

"Would you go out with him?"

"I don't know," I said carefully. "After all, Jeff, it's not as if you and I had a commitment."

Jeff looked funny. Concerned. "Come on, Tina, you know how I feel about you."

I felt bad. I really didn't want to hurt him. I forced a grin. "Don't look so serious," I said. "He just helped me with those forms. That's all it was and all it's going to be. Honestly, Jeff, you don't think I could fall for someone like that."

His anxious expression turned into a relieved one. "I didn't think so," he said almost smugly. "After all, you must realize why he's suddenly so interested in you."

"And why is that?"

Jeff pulled a record out of a cover and placed it on the stereo. "Because he thinks you're going to be the next Miss Spring Valley, and it would be a status thing for him to date the school queen."

An irritable feeling rose up in me. "Oh, yeah?" I said coldly. "Did it ever occur to you that he may just like me for myself?"

Jeff turned and flashed me his best and biggest smile. "He's too dumb to appreciate you for who you really are."

Talk about mixed emotions. On the one hand, I was annoyed by Jeff's certainty, as if there were no way I'd like anyone but him. On the other hand, he was telling me that he appreciated me. And he was probably right about Dave. Jeff placed the needle on the record and gave me a cocky grin. He was playing our favorite song, a love song that had been popular back when we were in ninth grade. How could I stay angry when he was being so romantic?

"May I have this dance?" he asked with mock formality.

"Gee, I don't know," I replied coyly. "You'd better take your place at the end of the line."

We probably looked pretty funny, dancing in the middle of the living room. In fact, I know we looked funny because Dorie came in and started giggling like a maniac when she saw us. It killed the mood. Jeff looked at his watch.

"Wow, it's almost eight. I've got to run."

"Why so soon?" He was already putting on his coat.

"A couple of guys from the team are coming over to my place to work."

I followed him to the door. "Want to meet me after cheerleading practice tomorrow afternoon?"

"I'll try," he said, "but I can't promise. We've got debate right after school." I thought if I heard the word debate one more time I'd scream.

He paused at the door and looked at me earnestly. "You're not really interested in Dave Powers, are you?" He looked nervous, and I knew he deserved an honest answer.

"There's only one guy I'm interested in," I said softly. "I just wish he had more time for me."

He kissed me lightly on the cheek. "Thanks for the pizza, Mrs. Steele," he called out to my mother.

"You're welcome, Jeff," Mom called back from the kitchen.

"See you tomorrow," I said, and he left.

I didn't really feel like calling Dave back just then. It seemed like a two-faced thing to do after what I had just told Jeff. But I had said I would call. I was saved from an immediate decision when the phone rang. It was Ruth.

"Hi, what are you up to?" I asked.

Ruth groaned. "Having a battle with calculus. And the calculus is winning."

"You're not the only one who's having trouble," I said and told her about meeting Helen that afternoon.

"What's she like?"

"Nice," I said. "Serious, but she has a sense of humor."

"You don't think she has much of a chance, though, do you?" Ruth asked.

I knew what she was talking about. "I don't know," I said. "She's actually very pretty, or she could be if she'd do something with her hair. And she's got a good talent."

"What?"

"She plays the violin."

"So, have you come up with a talent yet?"

"Not really." I sighed. "Dorie thinks I should demonstrate a cheerleading routine."

"Hey, that's not a bad idea," Ruth said thoughtfully. "If you could come up with something clever, something with a lot of kicks and maybe a cartwheel, it could almost be like a dance."

"I guess so," I replied without much enthusiasm.

"We'll work on it," Ruth promised.

We chatted for a few more minutes, and then I figured I had stalled long enough. "I'd better go. Dave Powers phoned earlier, and I'm supposed to call him back."

Ruth whistled. "Wow, he's really interested in you," she said.

"No," I demurred, remembering Jeff's remarks, "I think he's just interested in Miss Spring Valley. You know what I mean?"

"Yeah," she admitted, "you're probably right. He *is* heavy into his image. And not your type, anyway. But it won't hurt to be nice to him, and *you* know what *I* mean."

"I suppose so." I sighed again. "But I'll tell you, Ruth, I wish this pageant were over with."

"It will be, soon enough," Ruth assured me. "And you can't tell me you don't want to win."

I was silent for a minute. "No," I said finally, "you're right. I can't tell you that." With that we said our goodbyes, and I proceeded to call Dave back.

The phone rang almost six times, and I was ready to hang up when Dave finally answered. "Yeah?" He sounded angry.

"Hi, Dave, this is Tina."

"Oh, yeah. Look, I'm watching TV, and I can't talk. You want to go out Friday night after the game?" I could hear the TV blaring in the background. His abrupt question took me by surprise, and I didn't want to answer immediately. "Come on, I've got to know, yes or no. I want to get back to the game." He sounded impatient.

"I'm sorry, Dave," I said, "I'm—I've got a date. Maybe some other time."

"Yeah, right, talk to you later." He hung up.

He had style all right.

Chapter Nine

After my last class on Monday, I stopped in the girls' restroom. Kay Thigpen was standing in front of the mirror, putting on gobs of lipstick. She nodded at me, and I nodded back. I didn't know her very well. But I knew she acted tough and could be pretty nasty.

"You hear the news?" she asked.

"What news?"

She carefully blotted her lipstick and started combing her hair. "Laurie Rich. She dropped out of the pageant."

"How come?"

Kay shrugged. "She says beauty pageants promote stereotypes of women. She's crazy."

"I don't know," I replied as I leaned over to adjust my socks. "Maybe she's got a point. I don't think we should be judged solely on our looks."

As I straightened up, Kay was looking at me as if *I* were crazy. "What else?" she asked. "I mean, in the long run, that's all that counts."

I pulled my hair back into a ponytail. "I still agree with Laurie, but I wouldn't drop out. I mean, this is just a fun thing, for charity."

Kay laughed unpleasantly. "Maybe that's all it is for you," she said, smirking, "but as soon as I get out of school, I'm going to be a model. And you'd better believe it won't hurt if I can stroll into a modeling agency and announce that I'm the former Miss Spring Valley."

I didn't quite know how to respond to that, so I just shrugged as Kay gathered her makeup and made her way toward the door. She almost collided with Vicki Gilligan, who was on her way in.

"Hey, watch where you're going," Kay snarled and brushed past her out the door. Vicki just glanced at her haughtily and joined me at the mirrors. Looking at both of us side by side in the mirror, I felt like a real mess.

"Hello, Tina," she said coolly, with a condescending smile.

"Hi," I said. "Did you know that Laurie Rich dropped out of the pageant?"

"I heard that," Vicki said, "and I can't say I'm sorry."

"Why?"

Vicki leaned closer to the mirror to apply her mascara. "She's supposed to be an excellent dancer, ballet or something." She snapped the mascara brush back into its holder and gave me a wink—or maybe she was just testing to make sure her mascara didn't smear. "And I could do without the competition."

I was tempted to tell her about Helen and her violin, but I bit my tongue. Actually I didn't want to continue the discussion. It was depressing. I didn't like all those girls looking at one another out of the corners of their eyes, trying to decide who was prettier and who had the better talent. And what was really beginning to upset me was the fact that I sort of understood how Vicki felt. Laurie's dancing probably would have put my cheerleading routine to shame.

As I gathered up my books and pom-poms and opened the door to leave, Vicki asked, "How's Jeff?"

I stiffened but managed to say, "Fine."

"I really must talk to him about helping me with my audition speech," she murmured.

I turned back to her, replied sweetly, "Why don't you do that," and strolled out.

I don't know why I let Vicki bother me, I thought to myself as I walked down the hall toward the gym. *I think I can feel pretty confident about Jeff's affection. As far as I'm concerned, my only real competition in that regard is nuclear disarmament.*

I ran into the locker room, changed my clothes, and charged into the gym. Most of the girls were already there, sitting on the bleachers or doing stretching exercises on the floor. I called out, "OK, let's warm up." We gathered in a semicircle, and I led them through a few simple routines. Ruth came rushing in, late as usual.

"Sorry," she gasped and joined the group.

"Go sit down and catch your breath," I ordered. Ruth nodded thankfully and plopped down on the bleachers.

Sometimes I think I'm at my best when I'm leading these practice sessions. In all modesty I have to say I'm good at managing things when I'm doing something I know I'm good at. Ruth once told me that I had a real talent for leading, that I could tell people what to do without sounding bossy, and that I could correct them without hurting their feelings.

"All right, team, I've got something new to show you," I announced when we finished warming up. I went through the new routine quickly so that they could get a sense of what it looked like.

"Oooh, that's too hard," Candy said.

"It looks a lot harder than it is," I assured her. "It's just the way the steps are combined that makes the routine complicated. Here, watch." I went through it again, slowly, and identified each step as I did it.

"OK, let's all try the first combination together," I said, and the girls followed me through the steps. Candy Robinson looked totally confused, and I had to go through it with her again and again. But an hour later even she was doing fine.

"OK, one more time," I called out. A couple of girls moaned. I gave them a quick pep talk about how great we'd look Friday night at the game. As we were going through it for the last time, I saw Jeff enter the gym. I gave a mental "hurray" and a higher-than-usual leap at the end.

"You're all terrific," I called out as we finished. The girls scattered, gathering up their books.

Jeff ambled over. "That looked really good," he said. He was smiling, but I felt that he was holding back something. "I have to get back to my meeting," he said. "I just wanted to see you for a minute." Ruth joined us just then.

"Oh, no—I left a book that I need in my locker," she said. "Hi, Jeff."

"Jeff has to get back to his meeting," I told her. "Why don't you go get your book and meet me at the gym door." Ruth dashed off, and I turned back to Jeff. He looked uncomfortable. I felt a little worried.

"That cheer looked good," he said again. Something was definitely bothering him.

"Thanks," I said. "We've got two new cheers worked up for the game Friday night."

Jeff looked down. "I'm sorry I won't see them," he said quietly.

I stared at him. "What's the matter?"

He looked up, his beautiful brown eyes meeting mine. "The coach has set up a practice debate with Riverside High Friday night. That's almost two hours away. I won't be back until around midnight."

I could feel myself shaking inside, and I didn't trust myself to speak. So I kept quiet.

"The coach says it's important and we need as much practice as possible before the tournament." His eyes pleaded with me to understand.

I knew I should, but I couldn't. "Couldn't you tell the coach you've already made plans for Friday night?"

Jeff shook his head. "I can't do that, Tina. This tournament's a big deal."

"And I'm not?" I asked. "You know, Jeff, this whole debate business is really starting to bug me."

Jeff looked irritated. "Look, Tina, you know how important this tournament is to me."

"Yeah, sure, I know," I said. "It's all you've been talking about. But we had a date, remember?"

"Sure, I remember. And I told you I'm sorry. But I thought you'd be a little more understanding."

"I'm sick of being understanding," I said hotly. "You know, you haven't been all that understanding about what's important to me!"

Jeff grimaced. "Surely you don't mean that silly pageant, do you?"

I stared at him, and I could feel my face going pale. "It may be silly to you, but it just so happens that it's not so silly to me."

Now Jeff was getting pale, too. "You've changed, Tina. I never thought you'd be the type who'd take a dumb contest seriously."

"Don't change the subject," I said, my voice rising. "The point is, we had a date, and now you're telling me you can't get out of one crummy practice session."

Jeff interrupted. "Hold on! I could probably get out of going to Riverside if I had a really important excuse. But be reasonable, Tina, it's just another football game."

"And I'm just another date."

"Now, Tina, you know—"

I wouldn't let him finish. "You think I'll always be here, don't you? Old reliable Tina! When you've got nothing better to do, I'll be waiting. Is that how you feel?"

"Then don't wait for me!" he shouted. "Look, if you can't even try to understand why this is important, then maybe we just don't belong together. Maybe we should call it quits right now!"

"Call what quits?" I said, my voice dripping with sarcasm. "You're the one who's always saying we shouldn't get serious!"

"And now I know I was right!" he shot back.

His reply stunned me. I could feel the tears burning behind my eyelids, and I was afraid I was going to cry. I whirled around and stormed out of the gym.

I could hear Jeff calling out to me, "Tina, wait," but I was sick of waiting. Why should I wait? Would Vicki Gilligan hang around, waiting for some guy to get a break in his busy schedule so he could take her out? If Jeff couldn't appreciate me, that was his problem!

Ruth was waiting for me at the gym door. She took one look at me and knew something major had happened. I'll say this for my best friend—she may be famous for her ability to talk nonstop, but she knows when to be quiet. So we walked in silence, me staring straight ahead at nothing, Ruth glancing at me every now and then, waiting for me to talk about whatever it was that had turned my face to stone.

That's how I felt, like stone. Numb. No feelings. It was as if I had put on a mask, and I knew if I took the mask off, all the hurt would come pouring out. And I wasn't ready for that. When we reached my house, the mask was still on. Luckily no one was home. Ruth and I went up to my room, sat on my bed, and quietly, un-emotionally, I gave her a blow-by-blow description of the confrontation. And I almost made it to the end of the story before my tears started.

Ruth was terrific. She let me cry without saying a word; she just kept handing me tissues. As the flood of tears slowly turned into an occasional trickle, I turned to her and said, "I don't know what to do. I love him, I know that. And I know he cares about me. Maybe he even loves me. No, he couldn't love me. If he really loved me, he'd want to be with me. I'd be more important than his stupid debate tournament."

I blew my nose and sighed. "But he's got a lot on his mind, too," I said, my voice quivering. "Everything's so confusing right now."

"What do you mean?"

"I don't know," I said. "Things used to be so simple. There was school and friends and cheerleading and Jeff, and everything was just fine. I felt important, special. Now I'm just so mixed up."

"Do you think that's because of the pageant?" Ruth asked.

"Partly," I admitted. "It's been other stuff, too. Like my parents bugging me about college. At least I could count on Jeff being with me. Now I don't even have him." I could feel the tears returning.

"You'll work it out with Jeff," Ruth said. "You two have had little arguments before, and you've always made up."

I shook my head. "We've never had a fight like this. He was angry, Ruth, really angry. And I was, too. The way he looked at me—as if he didn't even know me. Maybe he doesn't. Maybe I don't know myself." And I was crying again.

Ruth put her arms around me. "It'll be OK," she said sympathetically. "I know you and Jeff will get back together. Just give it time. Give yourselves a chance to cool down. Try to concentrate on something else for a while."

"Like what?" I mumbled into a tissue.

Ruth thought for a minute. "Like the pageant,"

she said. "Look, I know it's not all that important. I've been making a bigger deal out of it than you have. But at least it would give you something to think about, and it could take your mind off Jeff for a while."

"Nothing can take my mind off Jeff," I said.

"OK, look at it this way," Ruth said. "You say you think Jeff's been taking you for granted. Picture this. It's the night of the pageant. You're standing up there on the stage, your arms full of roses. Jeff's in the audience. Everyone's eyes are on you. You'll have his full attention. And he'll realize, once and for all, that you're the only girl in the whole world for him."

As depressed as I felt, I still had to smile at Ruth's dramatic description. But I also had to admit that she had a point. Jeff might not take the pageant too seriously, but if I won, he couldn't help but think I was pretty special.

I got up from the bed and went to the dresser. I stared at myself in the mirror. I was a mess. My nose was red, and strands of hair were falling out of my ponytail. But I wasn't seeing that reflection. I was seeing myself in a stunning dress, hair done beautifully—and a crown on my head.

It was as if a spark had been lit within me. I wasn't going to sit around crying and wringing my hands, waiting for Jeff to call and apologize. I'd *make* him come back to me. I'd make him realize I wasn't someone to ignore, someone to take for granted. I'd be Miss Spring Valley!

"I could win," I whispered under my breath.

"What?" Ruth asked.

I whirled around and faced her squarely. "I could win!"

"That's what I've been saying all along," Ruth said.

"But now I'm serious," I stated and paced the room. "Look, I know I'm not the most talented. I *am* pretty, and you know as well as I do this is basically a popularity contest."

"It's too bad the students themselves don't decide the winner," Ruth said. "Then, you'd win for sure."

Maybe, I thought. *But there are other ways.* Ideas began to occur to me. Suddenly I started feeling, well, maybe not ecstatic, but at least a tiny bit excited. I sat down next to Ruth. "I know who the judges are," I said. "I found out today." I ticked them off on my fingers. "There's Mrs. Evans, that's Howie's mother. And Howie's an old buddy; you know he'll tell his mom to vote for me. Mrs. Callahan's president of the PTA and Linda Callahan's mother. You don't know Linda, she's in the ninth grade, but I tutored her last year in math. Mrs. Callahan likes me because I finally got Linda to pass math. I had Mrs. Cohen for trigonometry last year, and I was her star student. Then there's Dave's father, because he's president of the Chamber of Commerce. And then somebody named Mr. Gordon. I don't know him, but he's vice-president of the Chamber of Commerce, so I bet he'll go along with whomever Mr. Powers chooses. So you see," I finished triumphantly, "I could win."

Ruth was looking at me uneasily—I guess she'd never seen me so determined. "Gee, you *are* serious," she said.

"Look," I told her, "if I become Miss Spring Valley, Jeff will have to realize I'm special, right?"

"I guess so," Ruth said. She was silent for a minute, and then she asked, "Did you call Dave back last night?"

I nodded. "He asked me out for Friday night after the game. I told him no because I thought I'd be going out with Jeff."

"Why don't you call him right now and tell him you've had a change of plans and that you're available?" Ruth suggested.

"I suppose I could do that," I said thoughtfully. "After all, if I want him to use his influence with his father, I'd better start buttering him up." I went into the hall and pulled the phone into my room.

Dave answered on the second ring. I tried to make my voice sound bright and casual. "Hi, Dave, this is Tina."

"Yeah?"

Hmmm, this wasn't going to be easy. "I'm just calling because, well, you see, I've had this change of plans and, well, I can go out Friday night after all."

"Too bad," he replied. "I guess this isn't your lucky day. I've already asked someone else out. Vicki Gilligan." *Figures,* I thought glumly. *Vicki must know Dave's father is a judge, too. Now I've probably lost that vote.*

"OK," I said lightly, "see you around."

"Wait a minute," he said. "It just so happens I'm free Saturday night. How about it?"

How about what? I thought, but I replied sweetly, "I'd love to get together Saturday night."

"Pick you up at eight," he said and hung up.

I groaned. "He's really so awful."

Ruth looked at me sympathetically. "Listen, Tina," she said, "maybe you shouldn't go out with him. If you really hate being with him this much, maybe it's not worth it. I'm sure you could win the pageant without playing up to the judges. Just work on your talent and appearance. You've already got the grades going for you."

"It's worth it," I said grimly. "Hey, you're the one who was all for my flirting like crazy with him so he'd get his father to vote for me."

Ruth shrugged and looked a little apologetic. "I know," she said, "but I think I was wrong. I mean, you seem pretty miserable about going out with him."

"Look," I said angrily, "you wanted me to win. Now *I* want to win. And I'm not using him, he doesn't *have* to go out with me, you know. And it's not as if I've promised to *marry* him or anything."

"But you're using him," Ruth argued. "You're going out with him so he'll get his father to vote for you, so you'll get to be Miss Spring Valley, so Jeff will see that you're special, right? You're using Dave to get Jeff."

I glared at her, but I couldn't think of a response. Because she was right! This wasn't like me at all. But I didn't care. I was saved from having to reply by the sound of my mother's opening the front door downstairs.

"Listen," I said quickly, "let's not talk about this anymore. It's all going to work out."

"OK," Ruth said, but she didn't sound convinced. We went downstairs and joined my mother and Dorie in the kitchen.

"Hi, girls," Mom said. "Hungry?"

"You bet," I replied with fake cheerfulness, though I wasn't hungry at all.

We had a snack, and Ruth left. I went back to my room and tried to concentrate on homework until dinner. Then, after dinner I said I still had a mammoth stack of work left to do and disappeared into my room. I felt so lousy I just wanted to be alone.

Later that evening my mother tapped on the door. "There's a good movie on TV," she said. "Want to come down and watch it with me?"

I looked up and tried to smile brightly. "Thanks, Mom, but I'm really beat. I think I'll turn in early tonight."

She looked at me closely. It's hard for me to hide things from her. She's always been able to read my face. "Something's bothering you," she said gently.

Yes, I wanted to scream, but instead I kept the smile plastered on my face and shook my head. "No, nothing, just tired, that's all."

"Well," she said, "sleep tight then. Pleasant dreams." She seemed reluctant to leave.

"Night, Mom," I said firmly, and she left.

I *was* tired, but once I got into bed I couldn't fall asleep. I couldn't stop thinking about Jeff, about our fight. My mind was a jumble of contradictory thoughts. I was angry at him, and yet, I missed him. He'd treated me badly, I thought, but he was the only boy I'd ever love. *I'll show him! When he sees me with that crown on my head, he'll be sorry. And then he'll appreciate me.*

But a little voice kept asking, "Do you really think Jeff cares whether or not you're Miss Spring Valley?" I resolutely pushed that thought out of my mind and waited for sleep.

Chapter Ten

It wasn't easy getting through that next week. I think I deserved an award for my performance. Looking at me, no one would have guessed anything was wrong. I managed to avoid meeting Jeff face to face, even in the one class we shared, history. Luckily it was a large class, and our seats weren't near each others. Jeff used to joke and say that he'd never be able to concentrate on the teacher if I sat too close. I dawdled in the restroom until just before the bell rang so that I wouldn't have to see him before we actually settled down, and I dashed out as soon as we were dismissed.

Also, I knew his schedule, so I knew where not to be at certain times during the day. And I dragged all my books around with me so that I wouldn't have to visit my locker—our usual meeting place between classes. Even though I knew he wouldn't be there waiting for me, I didn't want anything to remind me of him.

It was as if another person had taken over my body. Some stranger with the face of Tina Steele took notes in class, laughed with friends during lunch, flirted with guys she wasn't even interested in. I was absolutely determined Jeff would not know how hurt I was.

Once my history teacher was late, and I couldn't help but sneak a look over my shoulder to see what Jeff was doing. Vicki was leaning over his desk, her long, glossy hair practically hiding him from my view. I could hear her laughing. What were they joking about? *You don't care*, I told myself sternly. *You've got other things to think about. Like Miss Spring Valley.*

And I did think about it—a lot. I felt as if I were on the campaign trail, like a politician. I called the Callahans' one afternoon to ask Linda how she was getting along in math, and I offered to help her if she was having problems. I stopped to see my former trigonometry teacher, just to say hello and to tell her how much I was enjoying calculus. And whenever I saw Dave, I flashed my brightest smile and tried to look as though I had a wild crush on him.

All the time I felt absolutely awful, like the

biggest phony in the world. I almost hated myself. *And* I missed Jeff.

Our eyes did meet once, on Wednesday after history class. I turned away. I was afraid he'd see in my eyes how much I missed him. He called that evening, and I was coldly polite.

"I'm very busy, Jeff. I can't talk to you now."

"Tina, we have to work this out—" he started to say.

But I interrupted him. "There's nothing to talk about." And I put the receiver back into its cradle.

Hanging up that phone was one of the hardest things I'd ever done. Of course I wanted to talk to Jeff; I was dying to hear his voice. But I knew what would happen. He'd talk about the debate tournament and how important it was. He'd be understanding and reasonable. Well, I just wasn't ready to be understanding. I was angry and bitter, and before I'd even talk to him, I wanted to make sure he appreciated me. I wanted him to think of me as someone very, very special. Otherwise, we'd just go back to the same old relationship, and I'd be old reliable Tina. He had to want me more. He had to want me so much he'd put his other interests aside. Miss Spring Valley wouldn't take second place to a debate tournament, I told myself firmly. But all the time I ached inside.

Unfortunately my mother overheard the phone conversation. Normally she wouldn't have said anything. My mother honestly believes kids deserve privacy. She has never cross-examined me about my social life, the way some of my friends' parents do. But I guess my expression must have worried her.

"Tina, is there something you want to talk about?"

I made a feeble attempt at a smile. "No, Mom, nothing."

She hesitated, then said, "Honey, you know I don't want to interfere in your personal life, but you haven't been yourself the past couple of days. You've been hiding out in your room, not saying much."

I tried to keep the annoyance I was feeling out of my voice. "Please, Mom, just don't worry. Jeff and I had a little argument, that's all, and I really don't feel like talking about it."

My mother nodded, but there were still lines of concern on her forehead. "Well," she said, "I hope you two work it out."

By the end of the school day on Friday, I was mentally exhausted from maintaining my act. Honestly, by then I could have challenged Vicki Gilligan for the lead in any Drama Club production. I was grateful that we had a football game that night. I'd have to concentrate on cheering, which wouldn't leave room for me to think about anything else.

We won the game. All the kids were jumping up and down and hugging each other, so I was able to slip away without anyone's noticing. I wasn't going to Patsy's party. Ruth had asked if I wanted to go with her and her date, but I wasn't in a party mood. I didn't feel like acting cheerful and pretending I was having fun.

At the same time, I didn't much feel like going home and sitting in my room alone. My parents were out for the evening, and Dorie was at a pajama party. It was funny. I didn't want to be alone, but I didn't want to be with a bunch of people, either. Mom had let me take her car to the game, so I headed out to the parking lot. As I walked outside the stadium, I was surprised to see Helen Davis standing in line outside the phone booth. She waved when she saw me, and I stopped to say hello.

"I didn't expect to see you here," I said.

She indicated the short, freckle-faced boy standing in front of her. "I think I told you my brother Joey plays in the marching band. I have to admit I'm not too crazy about football, but I did want to hear the band."

"Are you calling for a ride home?"

She nodded. "My mother was with us, but she got beeped."

I raised my eyebrows. "Beeped? That sounds like she was zapped by space invaders!"

Helen laughed. "She's a doctor, so she has to carry a beeper around in case there's an emergency. It went off in the middle of the game, and she had to go see a patient at the hospital."

"Well, look," I said, wanting company, "I've got my mother's car here. I could drop you and your brother off."

"Gee, that would be great," she said. "Come on, Joey."

It was a short ride from school to Helen's house. I have to concentrate when I drive, so we didn't say much.

"That's the house there," Helen said, pointing. As I pulled up to the curb, she got out, let her brother out of the backseat, and then turned back to me. "Would you like to come in and have some hot chocolate?"

I hesitated, then thought about my own empty, lonely house. "Hot chocolate sounds great," I said. I parked the car and followed her into the house.

Helen introduced me to her father, who was reading in the living room. Her brother headed for the TV. We took orders for hot chocolate and went back into the kitchen to fix it.

"I still can't thank you enough for helping me with calculus last Sunday," she said as she filled the kettle. "We had a pop quiz on Monday, and I never would have passed if you hadn't explained those problems to me."

"I'm glad I could help," I replied. "Did you finally choose a piece to play for the pageant?"

"I've narrowed it down to two possibilities," she said. Then she asked hesitantly, "I don't suppose you might want to listen to them and help me choose? They're both very short," she added.

"I'd like to very much," I said. "I don't know anything about classical music, but I'd love to hear you play."

Helen looked pleased. We fixed the hot chocolate, delivered mugs to her father and brother, and took ours upstairs to her room. Her violin case was lying on her desk, and as she took the instrument out and began to tune it, her face seemed to change. Her expression became focused and intense. When she began to play, her face took on a glow, and she looked as if she were alone in an enchanted world. The music she played was a lullaby, sweet and gentle. By the time she finished, I felt almost as transfixed as she looked.

"That was breathtaking," I said.

"Thank you," she said gravely. "It's one of my favorite pieces. The next one's very different."

She smiled and began a lively dance. I was amazed at how fast her bow moved across the violin. She finished with a flourish and looked at me expectantly. "Which do you think is better?" she asked.

I thought for a minute. "I like them both," I said, "but I guess I liked the first one better. Still, for the pageant, the second one might be a better choice. It's flashier, if you know what I mean."

She nodded. "That's what I thought. I liked the first one better, too, but because the second one is faster, it looks more difficult, and that could impress the judges."

"You're probably right," I agreed. I was thinking that this was all very strange. If I wanted to win so badly, why was I giving my competition advice?

Helen's expression matched the tone of my thoughts. She looked disturbed. Then she said, "I'm not happy about the Miss Spring Valley contest. I don't like what it's doing to me."

"What do you mean?" I asked, puzzled. She seemed as though she was doing just fine to me.

"I've never liked competitions," she said. "I don't like the idea of trying to beat somebody else. And I know this kind of high-school pageant isn't very important, but for the dumbest reason, I want to win. The talent part," she added hastily. "I know I'm no great beauty."

"What's your dumb reason?" I asked.

She hesitated before responding. "I'm not like you," she said finally. "I've never been very popular at school. I guess it's my own fault, really. It's been my choice not to get involved in after-school activities."

I could tell Helen was feeling a little embarrassed about telling me this, but I was interested in what she was thinking. I wanted to hear more. "What does that have to do with the pageant?"

Again she hesitated before speaking. "What it boils down to," she said slowly, "is that I'd like people to know who I am. I've always felt so isolated at school, so out of touch with everything that's going on. Remember when I spoke to you in class? You didn't even know my name."

I had to admit she was right. "I'm sorry about that," I said honestly.

She smiled. "It's not your fault. I could have introduced myself a long time ago. I guess people like you sort of intimidate me."

I was truly astonished. "Why?"

"I'm not sure," she said. "I guess it's because you always seem so confident, so sure of yourself."

I almost laughed out loud. *Me? Confident? If*

only she knew! "It's funny," I mused, "the kind of vibes people give off. Believe me, Helen, I'm not at all that sure of myself." She seemed surprised to hear that. Suddenly I felt a desire to share some of my feelings with her. "I've got dumb reasons for wanting to win, too," I said, and I told her the whole story about Jeff.

Helen listened carefully, her expression sympathetic. "I think I can understand how you feel," she said, "but I sort of know how Jeff is feeling, too."

"What do you mean?" I asked nervously. I wasn't sure I wanted to hear anyone take Jeff's side.

"Well," she said carefully, "when I'm preparing for a recital, I have to concentrate really hard, and for a while the performance becomes the most important thing in my life. Everything else—family and schoolwork, no matter how important they are to me—takes second place. Maybe that's how this tournament is for Jeff."

"I don't like being in second place," I said.

"Nobody does," she replied. "But you've got to realize this is only temporary. After the debate is finished, I'll bet your relationship with Jeff will go back to normal."

"I'm not so sure about that," I said. "Jeff has so many things on his mind. After the debate he'll probably be writing away to colleges and reading catalogs and deciding which ones he wants to apply to next year."

Helen raised her eyebrows. "But isn't that only natural?" she asked. "That's on all of our minds. Aren't you starting to think about college, too?"

Well, that question opened up a whole new conversation. I told her about my fear of college and of leaving Spring Valley. And again my new friend listened sympathetically. "I don't think your feelings are unusual," she said. "Everyone gets nervous, thinking about leaving home and going into an unfamiliar environment."

"But it's different for people like you and Jeff," I argued. "You both have goals and ambitions. Jeff's passionate about studying law, and you've got your music. I don't have anything like that."

"You've got to be kidding!" Helen exclaimed. "I hardly know you, but I see how talented you are!"

"What do you mean?"

"You're a born teacher," she said. "The way you explained that calculus to me was incredible. No one's been able to penetrate my math block before! And I know you tutor people. I bet you're good at that. Even being head cheerleader, isn't that teaching? Don't you have to create and teach routines to the other girls?"

How strange. I'd never before thought of myself as a teacher. But she was right! I felt a funny little surge of excitement. "And I enjoy teaching, too," I said thoughtfully.

"Plus," Helen continued, "you've got a subject specialty, too. Doesn't the idea of teaching math appeal to you?"

"Sort of," I admitted. "I'm not sure. It's something I'll have to think about." There was definitely a little spark in the back of my mind that hadn't been there before.

"And another thing to remember," she continued, "is that you don't have to know exactly what you want to do before you go to college. In fact, that's what college is for, to give you a chance to study a lot of different subjects and see what you like best."

"So I could take a lot of math and some teaching courses and a whole bunch of other stuff and see how I feel in four years."

"Exactly," Helen said.

"I can't tell you how much better you've made me feel," I said sincerely. "I feel talented for the first time in ages."

"Speaking of which, what are you doing for your talent in the pageant?"

I felt peculiar telling her about my cheerleading routine. It seemed so shallow compared to her music. She was polite about it, but I could tell she wasn't too impressed.

"I know it's not very exciting," I said, "but I can't think of anything else. Maybe I'm a good teacher, but I can't very well get up on a stage and teach."

"I don't know," Helen said. "We'll have to think about it."

I liked the way she said "we." It made me feel as if we were in it together. I felt a sudden desire to help her, too. "You know," I said hesitantly, "before, you said something about not being a great beauty. Actually, you're very pretty, but maybe you should do something different with your hair."

"You think so?" she asked eagerly. "I've never been any good with my hair. Could you help me?"

I examined her critically. "You have beautiful hair," I said. "Maybe if you let it hang loose." Obediently Helen pulled out some hairpins, and gorgeous, shiny black hair cascaded to her shoulders. "Wow!" I exclaimed. "You look prettier already!"

"My mother has a curling wand," she offered.

"Then let's experiment," I said.

We spent the next hour trying different styles, all the time laughing. After we found a hairstyle we both liked, we started on her makeup. In the midst of all this, Helen's mother came home. We went downstairs to show her Helen's new look.

"You look lovely!" she exclaimed. "Tina, you're a young lady of many talents. Helen told me how you helped her with her calculus." The three of us sat around talking until I happened to look at a clock.

"Yipes! It's almost midnight," I said. "I'd better get home."

As I stood up, Helen's mother said, "I'm so glad to see you girls aren't competitive about this beauty pageant. I must say, I really have doubts about the value of this experience."

I couldn't think of a way to respond to that; so I just said good night, and Helen walked me out to the car. "This has been fun," she said.

I agreed but added, "I wish your mother were right about what she just said. I do feel competitive. The pageant seems to have become very important to me."

Helen didn't say anything, only nodded in an understanding way as we stood by the car.

"The thing is," I said slowly, "I really want to win."

Helen smiled. "Then I hope you do."

Chapter Eleven

Throughout the next week, it was as if an epidemic had hit the school. I guess you could call it Miss Spring Valley fever. When I had gone out with Dave Saturday night, he had warned me about it. We had gone to hear some local rock band. The music was awful, or maybe the auditorium was just too small. Anyway, all I could hear were the drums banging out a monotonous boom-boom-boom and a lot of screaming. Pleading a headache, I convinced Dave to leave, and we ended up in a coffee shop. Naturally the conversation turned to the pageant, which was less than two weeks away.

"You'd better get psyched up for the next week and a half," he said in a rather pompous, know-it-all voice. "It's not going to be easy."

"What do you mean?"

He grinned unpleasantly. "Look I've seen the way you girls can get when you're competing with each other. It got pretty vicious last year." I didn't like the way he said "you girls." "Last year three girls dropped out because they couldn't take the pressure," he continued.

"I just thought they didn't want to be in it any more," I said, bewildered by this whole conversation.

He gave me a withering look. "No, idiot, they couldn't take all the nasty cracks from the other girls, people whispering behind their backs, that sort of thing. Man, you girls really know how to sharpen the claws."

"Don't say 'you girls,' " I retorted sharply. "And I'm not like that. Neither is Merrill Dellinger or Helen Davis."

"Who?"

"Helen Davis. She's the Latin Club nominee."

He brushed that away. "Who cares about her?" he said. "Latin Club candidates are always dogs."

"Helen's not a dog," I said hotly, "and that's not the point. Most of us are just not like that." *Except for maybe Kay Thigpen or Vicki Gilligan*, I thought to myself.

He gave a snide chuckle. "That's what you think now," he said. "Just you wait."

On Monday afternoon I found out what he meant. I was in the restroom, brushing my hair. Kay Thigpen and Lucy Morelli, Donna's younger sister, were there, too. Kay started giving Lucy a hard time.

"What's Donna doing for her talent, Lucy?"

Lucy grinned proudly. "She's showing how to make a quiche. Donna's a great cook."

Kay snorted. "That's really cute. I'm sure the judges will be overwhelmed at the sight of Donna beating eggs." The sarcasm in her voice was unmistakable.

"Cooking well *is* a talent," Lucy said.

"Yeah," retorted Kay, "but who's going to know Donna's a good cook? For all the judges know, that quiche could taste like garbage."

I was trying to stay out of the conversation, but Lucy looked so hurt that I couldn't stand it. I gathered up my books and patted her on the shoulder. "I think Donna's talent is terrific," I assured her. "I wish I had thought of it first."

Then I turned to Kay and gazed at her critically. "You'd better put a little makeup on your neck, Kay. You've got so much on your face, that your neck's a different color."

I marched out triumphantly, leaving Kay frantically examining her neck in the mirror. I knew with that comment I was sinking to her level, but I figured I had to. I just hated to see Kay giving Lucy a hard time.

There was another incident that day. I was at my locker when a senior I barely knew stopped by. "I hear you've been hanging out with Dave Powers recently," she said, smiling in a fake way.

"I wouldn't call it hanging out," I replied carefully. "I've only gone out with him a couple of times."

Her smile got bigger and faker. "Well, just don't fool yourself into thinking he's going to help you win that title," she said. "It takes more than good contacts to get to be Miss Spring Valley." And with that bit of wisdom, she walked away.

What a nasty thing to say, I thought. I wondered whom *she* was supporting. In the back of my mind, though, I knew there was more than a bit of truth in what she'd said.

Tuesday was worse. In my English class, we were divided into groups of three to discuss a poem. By some freak chance, I found myself with Patsy McCoy and Marcia Jacobs, both candidates, both nice people. We'd always been casual friends before. But now we were uncomfortable with one another, polite but cold.

118

Something really creepy happened the next period in history. The teacher, Mr. Spencer, is the sarcastic type, and sometimes he makes little cutting remarks about how immature we are. Usually no one pays attention. This time was different. I guess the class must have seemed restless because he stopped in the middle of a lecture and said, "I suppose it's unrealistic to ask you to concentrate on something as trivial as World War One when you've got something as important as the Miss Spring Valley contest to think about." His voice dripped with sarcasm. *Knock it off*, I thought, but he continued.

"I imagine some of you young ladies are positively fraught with anxiety as the great day approaches. But would you mind putting your excitement and trepidation aside for the next forty-five minutes and direct your attention to the subject at hand?"

He'd barely finished the last sentence when Candy, looking positively ill, jumped up from her seat and ran out of the room. Everyone, including Mr. Spencer, looked startled. There was a buzz of excited whispers until Mr. Spencer raised his hand for silence.

"Tina," he asked, "would you please go see if Candy needs some help?" I was glad to get out of the room, and I was concerned about Candy.

I'd never seen her do anything so dramatic before. I found her crying in the bathroom.

"Candy, what's wrong? Are you sick?"

Through her sobs, I could only make out a few words, something about her mother and the pageant.

"Calm down," I said. "I can't understand what you're saying."

Finally her tears subsided, and the story poured out. Her mother was excited about Candy being in the pageant because *she* had been Miss Spring Valley twenty years before. Bobby kept saying how he'd be so proud of her if she won, but she felt sure she couldn't win because her grades were so low. She said she didn't really care whether or not she won, but she'd talked to Marcy Nolan, last year's winner, and Marcy made her feel even more nervous.

"What did Marcy tell you?" I asked curiously.

Candy sniffed and blew her nose. "I showed her the long dress I was planning to wear, and she said it was too sophisticated and the judges wouldn't like it. Then she said I should put a rinse on my hair to make it darker so that it would look natural. I told her my hair color *is* natural, but she said it doesn't *look* natural."

I glanced at my own reflection in the mirror. Thank goodness my hair looked natural.

"Anyway," Candy continued, still sniffing, "everyone's getting me so nervous about it that it's no fun anymore. My mother will be upset if I don't win, and Bobby will probably break up with me."

"Don't be silly, Candy," I said briskly. "Your mother might be a little disappointed, but it won't really matter to her. And if Bobby really cares about you, it's certainly not going to make any difference to him whether or not you win." I felt like a walking contradiction. On the one hand I was trying to win so I could impress Jeff; on the other hand, I was telling Candy it wouldn't matter to *her* boyfriend.

She was calmer by the time the bell rang and we left the restroom. She ran on ahead of me, and I bumped smack into Jeff. We stared at each other for a minute.

Then Jeff asked, "How's Candy? Is she OK?"

"She'll be fine," I said. "She's just been getting nervous about the pageant."

Jeff frowned. "It's too bad she has to get upset over something so unimportant."

"I've got to run," I mumbled and marched off, hoping the outside of me wasn't shaking like the inside. *Just you wait, Jeff,* I thought, *just you wait.*

Ruth came over that evening to help me practice for the pageant. It didn't go very well because I felt silly, and I had a feeling I'd feel even sillier doing the cheers in front of judges. Ruth tried her best to be helpful, but I could tell she wasn't overly enthusiastic about my talent.

"That's not bad," she said after each cheer until I wanted to scream.

"Stop saying, 'That's not bad,' " I said. " 'Not bad' isn't good enough!"

"What do you want me to say?" Ruth asked.

"Just don't say anything," I snapped, and then immediately I felt awful about the tone of my voice.

"Tina, I wish you wouldn't get so—so frantic about all this."

I knew if I responded to that, I'd say something I'd be sorry for later, so I just clenched my teeth and muttered something like, "See if this split looks straight."

By Wednesday the tension was almost unbearable. At lunch that day I noticed Patsy McCoy wasn't eating anything. I offered her half my sandwich.

"No, thanks," she said weakly. "I've been skipping lunch. I want to lose five pounds before the pageant."

I was amazed. Patsy's not the least bit fat. "You don't need to lose five pounds," I objected.

Patsy looked at me through narrowed eyes. "I suppose you'd be happier if I gained five pounds and looked awful."

I stared at her in astonishment. I've known Patsy for years, and we've always been friendly. Why would she say something like that? And it immediately dawned on me. Of course. We were in competition. So I just said, "Well, good luck," and let it go.

Ruth reported that Marcia Jacobs and Merrill Dellinger weren't speaking to each other. I was shocked. Marcia and Merrill had been inseparable since sixth grade.

"What happened?" I asked.

Ruth grimaced. "They were out shopping together yesterday after school for pageant dresses. They both ended up choosing the same dress, and they had a huge fight over who would get it."

"That's absurd," I said. "One of them could have found something else."

Ruth shrugged. "People are getting awfully tense about this thing." She paused and then added, "Even you, Tina."

"Don't be ridiculous," I said irritably. "I'm not tense. What makes you think that?"

Ruth looked uncomfortable, as if she were afraid to tell me what she really thought. "You just haven't been yourself," she said finally. "I know you say you're doing this to get Jeff back, but honestly, Tina, I wonder if you're going about this the right way."

"Why don't you just mind your own business?" I snapped and then immediately wished I could take those words back. Ruth looked stunned and hurt, and I felt like crying. "Oh, Ruth, I'm sorry," I murmured. "I didn't mean that, really I didn't. You're right, I *am* tense. I just miss Jeff so much."

The hurt look was fading from her face, and she managed a small but understanding smile. "I know," she said. "I just wish you could think of some other way to get him back. Can't you two sit down and talk it out?"

I shook my head. "He's really got to want me back. He's got to think I'm someone he can't live without. Then I'll be ready to talk." Suddenly I felt so tired. "Look, let's just not discuss the pageant anymore."

But that wasn't easy, since Spring Valley High was talking about little else. All day, every time I ran into anyone I knew, the questions would come. "What are you wearing? What's your talent?" And there were crazy, stupid rumors that Candy had had a total nervous breakdown, that Kay was going to blackmail some of the girls to get them to drop out, that Merrill's mother had tried to bribe the judges. And every time I ran into another candidate, I gave her the once-over. Was she prettier than I was? Did she have a better figure? Was her hair shinier? I was so preoccupied by the end of the day that I found myself almost halfway home before I realized I had left a textbook I needed at school. I ran all the way back.

As I retrieved the book from my locker, I heard a door slam across the hall. I turned around and saw Marcia Jacobs, her back to me.

"Are you OK?" I asked.

"No!" she said loudly, without even looking to see who was speaking to her. When she did turn and face me, her expression was hard and angry. "Take my advice," she said harshly. "Don't tell anyone what you're doing for a talent."

"Why not?"

"Because the word got around that I was singing a certain song. And now I just heard that someone else is thinking of doing that very same song. With a full orchestra recorded on tape!"

"Maybe it's just a coincidence," I suggested.

"Ha!" Marcia snorted. "I followed this pageant last year, and, believe me, some people will do anything to make the others look bad." And with that she stormed away.

As I walked toward the door, I frantically tried to think if anyone else could possibly be doing cheers. There was Candy, but she had so much trouble learning cheers that I didn't think she'd do them. Passing the corridor that led to the music room, I heard something that sounded familiar. It was the lullaby Helen had played for me. I followed the sound of the violin and found Helen alone in a practice room, lost in her music. Her back was to me, and she didn't hear me come in. When she finished, I applauded lightly and she whirled around.

"Tina, hi! You startled me."

"That sounded great," I said. "But I thought you were going to do the other one, the fast one."

"I was," she admitted, "but I decided to do the piece I really love, even if it doesn't impress the judges as much."

"You'll still impress them," I said.

She smiled. "Thanks. Hey, how does my hair look? I tried doing it the way you showed me." Her hair looked terrific, and I told her so. She had brushed it behind her ears, with a little curl at the bottom. It set off her high cheekbones. "Can I ask your advice on something?" she asked.

"Sure."

"Mom said I could have a new dress for the pageant, but I haven't the slightest idea what I should get. As you can see," she said, indicating her drab skirt and too-big sweater, "I've never paid too much attention to what I wear."

I thought for a minute. "Something simple," I said, "with clean lines, no frills, something sort of elegant."

Helen listened seriously and nodded. "Do you think we could go shopping together Saturday? My mother never has time on Saturdays, and I really don't trust my own taste."

"Sure," I started to say, then suddenly stopped. *What am I doing?* I thought wildly. If she looked any better, she could win! "Wait—I don't know about Saturday," I said hurriedly. "I'll call you. I've got to run now." And I dashed from the room, leaving behind a startled Helen.

Thursday was a nightmare. In English we got back a quiz we'd taken on Monday, and for the first time in my life I had gotten a C. Next to the grade, the teacher had written, "This isn't like you at all." That seemed appropriate, since nothing I had been doing lately was like me. It was a minor quiz, and I'd gotten all A's up until then, so it wouldn't affect my final grade too much. Still, just the thought of getting a C on a quiz frightened me.

Later that day I saw Jeff with Vicki in the cafeteria. They were laughing together. The sight of them upset me so much that I almost burst into tears. I left the cafeteria without eating.

I had PE next, so I went to the locker room early to change into my gym clothes. Two seniors were in there. They didn't see me come in, and they were talking about the pageant. Hidden by the lockers, I eavesdropped, knowing they'd get to my name sooner or later. And so they did. They had just finished eliminating Marcia Jacobs—"too short"—when I heard my name.

"Oh, yeah, the captain of the cheerleaders," one of them said. "She's got a chance, she's pretty cute. And I'll bet she's a real politician."

The other one agreed. "They tell me she's just the sweetest, but I hear she's been hanging out with Dave Powers."

The first one laughed. "Some girls will do anything for a little glory." The two of them left, and I sat very still, feeling even sicker than I had when I'd seen Jeff with Vicki.

Somehow I made it through the rest of the school day. I felt that I was holding my breath, trying to keep from exploding. When I got home that afternoon, my mother was in my room, leaving a stack of small books and pamphlets on my desk. She turned around when I walked in. "Oh, hi, honey, I was just leaving these here for you."

"What are they?"

She smiled brightly. "College catalogs. One of the women in my office has a daughter who went off to college this year, and she had all these catalogs lying around. They're from last year, so they may not be up to date, but at least they'll give you some ideas."

It was all too much, the pageant, Jeff, and now all this college stuff. I turned to my mother angrily. "You know I'm perfectly capable of getting my own catalogs, when and if I want them!" I exclaimed.

My mother was taken aback. "Tina, what's gotten into you? Please lower your voice."

"Look, Mom," I said, trying desperately to keep my voice at a normal level, "I've got a lot on my mind right now. I don't need anything else to think about."

"But, Tina, this is important—"

"Everything's important!" I said, my voice rising again. "I'm sixteen years old, and I'm perfectly capable of deciding what's important!"

"Tina, can't you tell me what's wrong?"

"Oh, Mother, please!" I was practically yelling

at this point. "Just—just mind your own business."

As soon as the words left my mouth, I knew I shouldn't have said them. I could see their effect on my mother; she looked angry, sad, and hurt. "All right, Tina," she said quietly and left the room, closing the door behind her. I threw myself on the bed and sobbed.

Chapter Twelve

I woke up on Friday with a terrible headache, the memory of my fight with my mother pounding in my mind. I knew I had to apologize. I dressed quickly and went downstairs to the kitchen. My dad was sitting at the table alone, eating breakfast. He looked up when I walked in.

"Your mother had an early appointment, and she dropped Dorie off at school along the way," he said. "You must be hungry without any supper last night. What do you want for breakfast?"

"Just a piece of toast," I said and put a slice of bread in the toaster.

"I understand you and your mother had a little spat last night," he said.

I nodded, not trusting myself to speak.

"She's worried about you," he continued, "and for that matter, so am I. You've been acting very out of character lately, Tina. Is something bothering you?"

I nodded again.

My father sighed. "Well, honey, your mother and I know that when you're ready to talk about it, you will. And we're not going to bug you about it. But it hurts us to see you looking so sad."

He was being so sweet that I felt like bursting into tears again. "Don't worry, Dad, it'll be OK," I managed to say. I gave him a quick peck on the cheek, quickly ate my toast, and left for school.

I got there early; the doors weren't even open yet. There was a solitary figure sitting on the steps of the side entrance. When I got closer, I realized it was Donna Morelli. She was hunched over, her chin in her hands, and she looked awfully depressed.

She glanced up as I approached. "Hi," she said, her voice expressionless. I sat down next to her, and we were both silent for a few minutes. Suddenly she said, "I'm thinking about dropping out of the pageant."

"Why?" I asked.

Donna shrugged. "I don't know. It's not the

132

way I thought it would be. Everyone's acting so strange."

I had a feeling I knew what she was talking about, but I wanted to hear more. "In what way?" I asked.

There was a pause. "I'm not sure," she said. "I thought this Miss Spring Valley thing would be fun and exciting, like homecoming or pep rallies. I thought the nominees would get to be closer friends and cheer each other on. Instead, everyone's getting nasty and conceited and catty. Everyone's so competitive! The whole business is making me feel sick."

I nodded, understanding what she was saying, but I was taken aback by her next remark.

"Even you, Tina," she said, looking at me directly. "You're not yourself. You've been acting like you're on a campaign or something. You're trying to buy the judges by being friendly." She sighed. "It's happening to me, too. We're all getting crazy." We were both quiet for a minute, then she asked softly, "Is it very important to you?"

"Yes," I said. Then, "No. Oh, I don't know, Donna, honestly. I'm awfully confused."

"Me, too."

Then I put my hand on her arm. "Don't drop out, Donna," I pleaded. "Let's see this thing through together. Maybe then we'll understand what it's all about."

Donna looked doubtful, then managed a small smile. "OK," she said and gave a little laugh. "After all, I've already driven my family nuts practicing my talent. They say if I make one more quiche they're going to start throwing eggs at me!"

People had begun to arrive at school by then, and the doors were opened. As Donna and I joined the crush in the hallway, I heard a voice call my name. A second later Dave Powers was beside us.

"Tina, I've got something to tell you," he said and then gave Donna a look that clearly said get lost.

Donna looked at him, then at me. I felt embarrassed, but I didn't say anything. "See you, Tina," she said lightly and disappeared into the crowd.

Dave grabbed my arm and pulled me to the side of the hall. "You don't look so good," he said. "You're sort of pale."

"Thanks a lot," I replied sarcastically.

"Look, Tina, I mean it," he said, ignoring the tone in my voice. "The pageant's less than a week away, and you've got to look terrific. Really healthy. Remember, the judges like girls who have that all-American look."

I sighed. "Is that what you had to tell me?"

He smirked. "You ought to be a little nicer to me. After all, I put in a good word for you with my old man."

I felt a little thrill run through me, and I put effort into a sweet smile. "Thank you, Dave."

"How's your talent coming along?"

The thrill disappeared. "It's OK," I said. "I think it'll do."

He looked irritated. "It can't just 'do,' Tina, it's got to be fantastic. Lively and upbeat, get it? You'd better work on it some more. When you do those cheers onstage, you want to be peppy and full of personality."

"I'll work on it," I promised, although I was beginning to feel sick again.

Dave grinned. "My father thinks I've got great taste in girls. Don't make me lose my reputation."

The bell rang, and I had an excuse to get away from him. But the sick feeling stayed with me all day. By the last period of the day, I felt so ill that I ran from class the minute I could and walked rapidly to the exit. I felt as though I were moving in a cloud. I was so dazed that I didn't hear Jeff calling my name.

"Tina, what's wrong?" he asked. His face showed concern.

"I don't feel so well," I blurted out.

135

"You don't look well," he said. For some reason, I didn't feel the resentment I had when Dave said the same thing.

"I—I want to go home," I said weakly, tears gathering in my eyes.

"I've got a car here," Jeff said immediately. "Come on, I'll take you home." He put his arm through mine protectively and guided me out of the building. By the time we were in his car, I felt more under control.

"I appreciate this," I said formally, "but I don't want to take up your time. Don't you have a debate meeting?"

He brushed that aside. "Sure, but I can be late. You're more important than any meeting, Tina."

I sat very still. Did he mean it? My mind was in a whirl. I felt dizzy and more confused than ever before. I looked at Jeff in bewilderment, and he gave me a tiny smile. I glanced away quickly. I didn't know what to say, so I just stared at the floor for the short ride to my house.

When we got there, Jeff jumped out, opened the door for me, and tenderly walked me to the door. As we stood on the porch, he turned me toward him. "Tina," he said gently, "I think I know what's upsetting you. It's the pageant, isn't it?"

Through the haze in my eyes, I could see his face, caring and kind. I nodded.

"It's not worth it, you know?" he said.

"I know," I whispered, and as the words left my lips, I knew I was speaking the truth.

Just then the door opened, and my mother stood in the doorway. She must have heard the car pull up. "Tina, Jeff, what's wrong?"

I tried to say my usual "Nothing, Mom," but the words were buried in tears. I heard Jeff say something about calling later, and the next thing I knew I was sitting with my mother, crying while she silently handed me tissues. Between the tears, I told her everything.

Mom kept hugging me and saying things like "I know" and "I understand." My sobs subsided at last, and as I blew my nose, I had a strange, comforting sensation of relief at finally letting all·those tears flow.

"You know, Tina," Mom said, "when I was in college, my best friend and I were both candidates for homecoming queen. We laughed about it at first and swore that it wouldn't affect our relationship. But as the big day approached, we started feeling the pressure. Our friends in the dorm started taking sides, as if the two of us were in a struggle. But the night before the big homecoming game, we had a heart-to-heart talk.

We realized that nothing was more important than our friendship."

"Who won?" I asked.

My mother laughed. "Some girl whose name I can't even remember."

I leaned back in the chair and took a deep breath. "Deep inside, Mom, I know it's not important. So why have I been getting so crazy?"

My mother smiled. "Maybe you need something to make you feel special. Every now and then we all need to show the world that we're important."

It was all beginning to make sense. "Now I can see what an idiot I've been. I was so scared and worried that Jeff would find someone or something he liked more than me. But Jeff doesn't care if I'm Miss Spring Valley. If he did, he'd be just like Dave. All I wanted was for Jeff to appreciate me. But I know becoming Miss Spring Valley is not the answer."

"You are special," Mom said firmly, "to Jeff, to your family, to your friends. You're special because you are who you are, not because of some title."

I felt so much better. It was as if an enormous burden had been lifted from my shoulders. I could see that all along I had been uncomfortable with the way I had been feeling, with the way I—and so many others at school—had been acting. But—there was still the pageant.

"Maybe I should drop out," I said.

"I don't know if that's necessary. After all, it *is* for charity. And after all you've been through, you might as well have the glamour of the evening. I think it's just a question of how you feel about it, how much significance it has for you."

"I really don't think I care whether or not I win," I said, and I was glad that I could say that honestly.

"Good!" my mother said approvingly. "Then you might as well finish up this experience and have an evening to remember. And, of course," she added slyly, "it's a pretty good excuse for a new dress!"

"Hey, that's right!" I said happily. "Can we go shopping tomorrow? Helen Davis wants to get a dress, too. She could come with us."

"Sounds like fun," Mom said. "We'll have a real shopping expedition. What time do you want to go?"

I thought for a minute. "Well, we have a pageant rehearsal in the morning, just a run-through to see what order we're in. We don't have to do our talents or anything; so we should be finished by noon."

"Great," said Mom. "I'll pick you girls up at school, and we'll go out to the mall for lunch. Then we can spend the afternoon shopping."

I gave her a hug. What a terrific mom!

"By the way," she added, "now that you and Jeff seem to be back on the road to romance, will he be your escort for the pageant?"

My mouth fell open, and I stared at her in horror. "Oh, no!" I yelped in dismay. "I forgot all about needing an escort! I've got to call him."

Just then the phone rang, and once again I thought I just might have ESP. It was Jeff. "Tina, I'm still at school," he said, "but I wanted to call and see how you were feeling."

I felt warm all over. "Much better," I said. "And, Jeff, I just want to say, I'm sorry about everything."

"I am, too," he said. "For the last week, I've felt like there was a big, empty place in my life. I've missed you so much, Tina. Can we pick up where we left off?"

"I hope so," I said. "Listen, I know how you feel about the pageant, but would you like to be my escort, anyway?"

Jeff groaned. "Tina, I'm sorry. Vicki Gilligan asked me to escort her, and since I didn't think you wanted to see me ever again, I said yes." But before I could feel a tiny twinge of jealousy, he added, "I really didn't want to go with her, she's so phony. To be honest," he said, and he laughed in a slightly embarrassed way, "I only said yes so I could be there and see you. Are you angry?"

"No," I said truthfully, "it's my own fault for not asking you sooner."

"I wish I could see you this weekend," he said, "but I have to go out of town with my folks to see my grandparents. They're insisting I go. You're not the only one who thinks I'm spending too much time on debate!"

"That's OK," I said. "I've been getting behind at school, and I need to spend the weekend catching up."

"I know it's none of my business," Jeff said, "but, just out of curiosity, who are you going to ask to be your escort?"

Reluctantly I replied, "I guess I'll have to call Dave Powers."

Jeff sighed. "Too bad we can't switch partners. I think Dave and Vicki would make a perfect couple."

I laughed. "You're probably right. Maybe after the pageant we can point them in the same direction!"

After we hung up I decided to call Dave right away and get it over with. "Dave? Hi, this is Tina."

"Yeah?" What a great conversationalist.

I took a deep breath. "Would you like to be my escort for the pageant?"

"Well, it's about time," he drawled. "I've been wondering when you'd get around to asking me." I gave a silent shudder and proceeded to arrange details with him. Afterward I joined my mother in the kitchen. She had just taken some cookies out of the oven and was setting them out to cool.

"Well, Jeff's already got a date for the pageant, so it looks like I'll be going with Dave."

My mother smiled sympathetically. "Too bad," she said, "but I imagine Dave will enjoy being part of the show."

"That's true," I said, "and after all, it's not as if it were a major event." Mom gave me a quick hug and handed me a warm cookie. For the first time in a week, I was ravenous.

Chapter Thirteen

I arrived at the school auditorium Saturday morning about fifteen minutes early, and only about half a dozen girls were milling about. I saw Donna Morelli sitting alone, so I went over to her.

"I'm glad you're here," I said, sitting next to her.

She smiled. "I decided to stick it out. After forcing my family to eat quiche for a week, I thought I might as well go through with it. I can't say I'm particularly enthusiastic about it, though."

"Me neither," I replied.

Donna looked surprised. "I thought you were really into it," she said.

"I did get carried away," I admitted. "To be honest, I don't know what got into me."

"I know what you mean," she said. "I found myself thinking it was all much more important than it really is."

I nodded energetically. "Me, too. But I feel much better about it now." We smiled at each other in understanding.

The others had come in by then, and I saw Helen standing alone near the door. I waved for her to come over. She looked a little uneasy, and I remembered I hadn't been too friendly the day before.

"My mother's picking me up after rehearsal this afternoon to go shopping for a new dress. Want to come?"

Her face lit up. "I'd love to." She looked around nervously. "What do we have to do today?"

"Nothing much," I assured her. "Just walk through the program and see where to stand."

Just then we heard a shrill whistle coming from the direction of Lynn Pickens, the senior class president. "OK, everyone," she called, "can we all gather here at the front of the auditorium?"

I passed Candy Robinson as we moved toward the front. "Isn't this exciting!" she said, practically bubbling over. She had obviously recovered, too.

"All right," Lynn said as we all took our seats

144

at the front, "this is how it goes. You'll all be backstage in alphabetical order. One at a time you'll walk out to the center of the stage and have ten seconds to say your name. Let's try it."

We straggled up to the stage. It took awhile to get us in alphabetical order, and poor Lynn practically had to scream to be heard above the chattering. "People, please!" she yelled. "Remember who's in front of you."

I mentally noted Candy's blond curls in front of me. Wait, those curls looked a little less blond than usual! "Candy," I whispered, "did you do something to your hair?" Candy turned and gave me a little giggle. "I decided maybe I should listen to Marcy's advice—I put a rinse on it."

I sighed. It was all beginning to seem so ridiculous.

"Now," Lynn said once we'd all crossed the stage, you'll have five minutes to change into costumes. This time, you'll go in reverse alphabetical order."

"Gee, this is getting complicated," Candy murmured.

"You'll each have five minutes to perform," Lynn said. "We're not actually doing the talents today; so I just want you to go on to the stage, in order, and describe your talent."

Kay went out on the stage. "I'll be modeling an original outfit I made myself that can be worn in different ways. It'll start out looking like a suit. First, I'll take off the jacket, and then it'll look like a school dress. Then I'll take off the shirt, and there'll be a little strapless camisole under it so that it'll look like a sun dress. Then I'll take off the skirt, and there'll be shorts underneath. I'll be doing this to music."

"Sounds like a striptease," someone muttered.

Lynn looked worried. "Kay, uh, this has to be, you know, respectable."

Kay shot her a withering look. "Don't worry," she snarled. "All the best parts of my body will be covered."

It was my turn next. In the three seconds it took me to get to the center of the stage, I knew I wasn't going to do a cheerleading routine.

"I—I'm going to talk," I said.

"Talk about what?" Lynn asked.

I thought rapidly. There was something vague forming in the back of my mind, and I was grateful that I still had about five days to figure it out. "About—about math," I said, "and—and life." I ignored the laughter coming from the side of the stage.

"Well, OK," Lynn said doubtfully. "Next." As

Candy pranced toward the center of the stage, I walked back on a cloud. I didn't know exactly what I'd be doing, and yet I felt lighter already. I passed Helen on my way to the back of the line, and she flashed me a thumbs-up sign.

When we finished stating our talents, Lynn said, "OK, after this you'll have five minutes to change back into your dresses. By this time your escorts will also be backstage. The emcee will call you one at a time, and you'll come out on the stage with your escort. Then the emcee will ask you a question. This is for points on poise and confidence."

"What kinds of questions?" someone asked.

"No big deal," Lynn assured her. "Just stuff like 'Who's the biggest influence in your life?' and 'How can people make this world a better one?' "

"He won't ask anything hard, will he?" Candy asked anxiously.

Lynn rolled her eyes and shook her head. "Finally," she said, "when this is finished, you'll all be onstage with your escorts. The judges will make their decision. First, the emcee will announce the winner of the talent category. Then he'll announce third, second, and first runners-up. Then there will be a drumroll, and he'll announce Miss Spring Valley. As each winner is announced, she'll come to the front of the stage with her escort. OK? Got it?" We all nodded.

As I looked out into the auditorium, I noticed Ruth sitting toward the back. Lynn dismissed us, and I went over to her. "Hi! What are you doing here?"

"I just thought I'd see how you were doing," Ruth said. "I heard your talent announcement." She smiled broadly. "Whatever it is, it sounds better than cheerleading."

I plopped down next to her. "I'm glad you're here," I said. "I want to tell you I'm sorry I've been so obnoxious this past week."

Ruth leaned over and squeezed my hand. "And I'm sorry for nagging you about this pageant," she said. "I guess I got carried away with the excitement. It's not really that big a deal, is it?"

"It sure isn't," I agreed. "Listen, Mom's coming to take Helen and me shopping for dresses. You want to come with us?"

"Sure," said Ruth.

Helen came over, and the three of us went out to the parking lot to wait for my mother, passing Vicki on the way. Luckily, I hadn't been near her during the rehearsal; therefore, we hadn't exchanged any words. When our eyes met, we both flashed big fake smiles.

"Your talent sounds interesting," she said, though her tone suggested she thought it was anything but. I thanked her politely. "Who's escorting you?" she asked, a wicked gleam in her eyes.

"Dave Powers," I replied, and then I couldn't help but say sweetly, "Jeff told me he's going with you. We're very, very close, you know."

"Oh," Vicki said, trying to act as though she weren't surprised.

"See you later," I said airily and strolled away with my friends, leaving Vicki behind with her mouth open.

"What's that all about?" Ruth asked.

Outside, I told her and Helen the whole story. "I'm still a little worried," I admitted. "I know Vicki's going to look terribly glamorous, and she'll probably knock herself out flirting with Jeff."

"From everything I've heard about Jeff," Helen said, "he doesn't sound like the kind of guy who would fall for that routine."

"I hope you're right," I said nervously. "Look, there's my mother."

We had a wonderful afternoon. Mom treated us all to lunch, and we entertained her with an exaggerated description of the rehearsal. Then we hit the shops. Between Helen and me, we must have tried on about fifty dresses.

"How does this look?" I asked, modeling a simple blue-gray crepe dress with small cap sleeves.

Mom looked at me critically. "It's a gorgeous dress," she said, "but it doesn't fall right on you."

"Could I try it on?" Helen asked. When she put it on, we all gasped. It was perfect for her.

"You look absolutely elegant," Ruth said.

Helen struck a pose. "Hollywood, here I come," she declared, and we all laughed. We finally found a dress for me, too, silky pink fabric with a fitted waist and puffy sleeves.

By the time we had made our purchases, we were all hungry again. "Now it's my turn to treat," I said, "and I think we've all earned a sundae."

"I'm glad the rehearsal's over with," Helen said as we wolfed down our ice cream. "I feel so much more relaxed about the whole thing."

"I wish I could relax," I said. "Now I have to go home and write my talent." Mom looked puzzled, and I told her how I'd decided to change my presentation. She seemed pleased.

"Sounds intriguing," she said. "But how are you going to combine math with life?"

"I'm not sure," I said thoughtfully, "but I think it will have something to do with being logical, looking at all the options, and trying out different possibilities."

"Well," Mom said, smiling, "that certainly sounds profound."

"It won't be flashy," I said, "and I doubt if I'll get any points for it, but it's something I want to do. Oh, and don't let me forget, Mom, I have to make an appointment with the guidance counselor Monday morning."

"What for?" asked Ruth.

"I have to start thinking about colleges. I want to find one that has a good math department but that's also strong in other subjects," I said, smiling at Helen. "Right now I think I want to be a math teacher, but I want to check out a few other fields, too."

Mom looked really pleased. She put her arm around me and gave me a squeeze.

"That's great," Ruth said. "You've always been terrific in math."

"And," Helen added, "you're already an excellent teacher."

My mother agreed. "You couldn't be more sensible," she said. "And as for being a math teacher, it's a perfect way to combine your talents. As I've always said, Tina—"

"I know, I know," I interrupted, "I'm a lucky girl."

Mom smiled proudly. "You certainly are."

Chapter Fourteen

"Beautiful." My father stood in the doorway, watching me preen in front of the mirror.

I flashed him a grateful smile. "Thanks, Dad." I had to admit I looked pretty good. The pink dress was simple and feminine, and Mom's pearl choker added a touch of elegance. Mom and Dorie joined my father in the doorway.

"Honey, you look lovely," my mother said.

"Great!" Dorie cried.

My family's proud faces filled me with warmth. I had given them all such a rough time the past few weeks, yet there they were, beaming at me with love and support. What a fantastic bunch!

"What time is Dave coming for you?" asked Mom.

"Seven. But you guys don't have to be at the

auditorium until eight." I thought briefly how perfect everything would be if only it were Jeff picking me up instead of Dave. *Oh, well, live and learn*, I thought philosophically. At least Jeff and I were on the road to recovery. Still, there was a tiny bit of insecurity in my mind. After all, he would be spending the evening with Vicki, and I knew she'd do everything within her power to enchant him. But I firmly brushed those fears aside. Mom put the finishing touches on my outfit by lending me her pearl earrings and best evening bag. And as I gave myself a final look in the mirror, I heard the doorbell ring.

Dave looked great, very suave and sophisticated, and he gave me an approving glance as I descended the stairway into the living room. He thrust a long, thin box at me. "Here," he muttered in his usual gracious way. Cradled among tiny ferns was one long-stemmed pink rose.

"Dave, how lovely," I said. In spite of everything, he did have good taste.

"My mother picked it out," he replied. *Oh, well.*

To a chorus of "Enjoy yourselves" and "Have a wonderful time," we left.

As we walked to Dave's car, he stopped suddenly. "Hey, where's your cheerleading costume for the talent?"

I smiled serenely. "I'm not doing cheers, Dave, I changed my mind."

He looked at me suspiciously. "What are you going to do?"

"I'm giving a speech," I told him calmly. "It's called 'Mathematics: A Guide for Living.'"

"That sounds *serious*," he exclaimed in dismay.

"It is," I assured him and eased into the passenger seat.

He grumbled all the way to school, saying stuff like "too heavy" and "really stupid." I ignored him and studied the notes I had tucked into my mother's velvet bag. I'd worked very hard on the speech, and I was sure I had it committed to memory. Jeff had even given me some tips on presentation.

Dave was still complaining when we pulled into the parking lot. "Oh, shut up, Dave," I said good-naturedly. "I'm doing what I want to do, that's all there is to it."

The auditorium was empty, but there was a frenzy of excitement backstage where the candidates and escorts were milling about. Everyone looked terrific all dressed up. Candy looked adorable. Her pale blue dress set off her light blond curls. "Candy! Your hair's light again," I exclaimed.

Candy patted her hair. "I washed out the rinse," she said.

"Good for you!" I was glad she had realized Marcy's advice was silly.

Candy nodded. "Bobby likes it better this way." I sighed sadly. Would Candy ever learn to listen to herself?

Donna was dashing all around, precariously balancing a basket of eggs. "Where can I stash these?" she kept asking.

Poor Lynn Pickens, she was frantically trying to get everyone organized. A couple of Dave's buddies were also escorts, and he disappeared with them. I found Helen off in a corner talking quietly with a tall, thin boy with glasses.

"Tina, this is Stan Bleecker," she said. "Stan's president of the Latin Club."

"I must say," said Stan, adjusting his glasses, "this is all rather interesting. In a socio-cultural sense."

I didn't know what he was talking about, but I nodded agreeably. Helen looked radiant, and the blue-gray dress was perfect. Kay Thigpen strolled past us, and Helen and I rolled our eyes together. Kay had on the splashiest dress I'd ever seen, bright red with sequins on top, only there weren't too many sequins because there wasn't too much top.

Dave joined us then, though his eyes were following Kay. "Wow," he said, shaking his head. But his attention was immediately diverted by the next entrance backstage—as was everyone else's.

Vicki was walking in with Jeff. Of course my eyes were on Jeff, who looked awfully handsome, if a little uncomfortable. But everyone else was staring at Vicki. And when I reluctantly turned my eyes from Jeff, I could see why. She looked positively regal in her white satin gown. Her glossy black hair fell down her back in a cascade of curls. She held on to Jeff's arm possessively, and the sight of that gave me a little pang. It was getting crowded backstage, and soon I couldn't see them. It was just as well. I needed to concentrate on my speech.

We could hear the audience coming in by then, and the school band began tuning up. Lynn tried to hush everyone and introduced the emcee to us. He was a local celebrity, a popular disc jockey from a radio station. He made a couple of corny jokes and told us we were all potential Miss Americas. No one paid any attention to him. Then we heard the band strike up the Spring Valley High song, and Lynn waved her arms wildly. "OK, everyone, it's time!"

Like magic, silence filled the room. Helen and

I squeezed hands and took our places in line. We could hear the emcee out front telling more corny jokes and introducing the judges. "And now, ladies and gentlemen, I have the pleasure of presenting to you the gorgeous gals of Spring Valley High." *What a jerk*, I thought.

It all went smoothly, though, as each girl strolled onto the stage, announced her name, and walked off to the other side. Candy went before me and said her name with a giggle. I waited for a moment and followed.

There were bright lights on us, and I couldn't even see the audience, but I pretended I was looking straight at my family and smiled broadly. "Hi, I'm Tina Steele." Well, that part was easy enough.

Once we were all backstage again, most of the girls started changing into talent costumes. We had left the escorts in the wings on the other side, so we had some privacy. There was less noise than I'd expected. I think at this point, we were all so keyed up we couldn't speak. I didn't have to change my clothes, so I sat in a corner going over my speech one last time. I was glad we were performing in reverse alphabetical order this time. I'd be second, right after Kay, and I could get it over with.

I felt sort of sorry for Kay. She danced around

on the stage peeling off her clothes and struck a pose in the little playsuit she'd ended up wearing. But then she had to pick up the clothes she'd taken off, which spoiled the effect.

And then I heard my name. I felt as if I were walking in slow motion, but somehow I made it to the center of the stage. I took a deep breath and began.

"Frequently people are surprised when I tell them my favorite subjects in school are mathematics—algebra, geometry, and calculus. They ask me, 'How can numbers be so fascinating?' But I think there's a special relationship between math and life. It has to do with logic, with cause and effect, with action and consequence. An equation is like any problem we encounter in life. There are several ways to approach it, and if one possibility doesn't work, we try another."

My voice was sure and strong. Everything I was saying sounded natural, as if I were just talking to a friend, instead of reciting a speech I had memorized. By the time I approached the conclusion, it seemed as if only a few seconds had gone by, although I knew from countless practices that the speech was exactly five minutes long.

"In life we gather together with friends to

share happiness and multiply our joys. And together we share our problems and sorrows, and divide them. Life can be bewildering and confusing, just like math. But with friends, and parents to guide us, and by developing wisdom and maturity, we can work toward reaching logical and satisfying solutions."

I barely heard the applause as I gave a little bow and walked backstage to where the escorts were waiting. The first person I saw was Jeff. He was smiling and silently clapping his hands. I smiled back and made my way over to Dave. He was leaning against the wall, and yawning. I didn't care. The hardest part was over, and now I could relax and watch the others.

Candy did a tap dance. It wasn't very good. She seemed to be having difficulty following the beat of the music. But she did look cute, her curls bouncing up and down.

Donna's quiche demonstration started off with a bang. "This recipe calls for five eggs," she began. "It's important to crack your eggs properly," she was saying when the egg she held slipped from her hand and fell to the floor.

I think I would have passed out right then and there, but I have to hand it to Donna, she made a rapid recovery. She shrugged her shoulders, and said, "Nobody's perfect. And if you reduce the other ingredients, you can make this quiche with only four eggs." Everyone laughed, and I silently cheered her poise.

Patsy McCoy went next with a hysterically funny clown routine. I laughed like crazy, but I didn't think the judges would vote for it. The big surprise was Marcia Jacobs, who belted out "Cabaret." She was great, very professional—and no one else sang her song. In all fairness I have to say that Vicki was awfully good, too. She wore a long, white, hooded cape over her dress and recited the balcony speech from *Romeo and Juliet*. Her voice was dreamy and romantic, and for a moment I could almost believe she was a sensitive, sincere, young girl wistfully reflecting on her new love. I just hoped it was Romeo she was pining for and not Jeff. Merrill displayed some paintings she'd done. They were beautiful up close, but I knew no one could see them clearly from the audience.

Helen played flawlessly. In the big auditorium the music sounded even better than it had in her bedroom or in the practice room. And if the applause was any indication, I'd say she had stolen the show.

Finally everyone was backstage again. Those who had to change had five minutes to do so, and those of us who didn't had a few minutes to breathe and change back into our dresses. Then it was time for the questions. We were lined up, with our escorts, in alphabetical order.

The first one out was Helen. She was asked, "Do you have any special career goals?" It was a perfect question for her, and she calmly and confidently described her musical ambitions.

Merrill got a tougher one. "If you were president of the United States, what would be your first priority?" She rattled off something about peace for all nations. When she returned backstage, she gave me a good-natured shrug and mumbled something about having heard that answer on the last Miss America broadcast.

When Jeff led Vicki out, I watched curiously. "What, in your opinion, is the most important quality in any relationship between two people?" Vicki struck a pose that made her appear to be thinking deeply. "I believe that sincerity is the most significant quality a person should aspire to. No relationship can succeed unless the people involved are honest with each other." I almost laughed out loud.

And so it went, a few silly questions—"Who's your favorite movie star?" —and a few unanswerable ones—"What is the greatest problem facing teenagers today?"

Poor Candy. She was asked, "Do you think relationships between boys and girls are different today from those of teenagers in your parents' generation?" She thought very hard, then smiled brightly. "Yes."

And finally it was my turn. I put my hand on Dave's arm, and we went out on the stage. The emcee beamed at me, took a card from his pocket, and read, "What have you learned from being in the Miss Spring Valley pageant?" Thoughts flowed through my mind. I knew what I *should* say if I wanted to win, something about gaining poise and making new friends. But I also knew what I really thought.

"The pageant can be a learning experience in many ways. But I don't believe it's good for people to compete with one another, especially for superficial reasons. Being a part of the Miss Spring Valley contest can be fun, but only as long as it's not taken too seriously."

I could see Lynn Pickens in the wings, her mouth open, and Dave gave me a look of total disgust. But from the other side of the stage, I could hear applause, and as I glanced over there, I could see Helen, Merrill, Donna, and a few others clapping their hands.

Once backstage again, we lined up with our escorts. "I'm sorry, Dave," I said almost sincerely.

"I know you were counting on escorting the next Miss Spring Valley."

"You really blew it," he growled. *Not in my mind*, I thought, feeling instead like a real winner.

One by one we were called out again, this time to find out who would be the next Miss Spring Valley.

"Ladies and gentlemen, the judges have reached a decision," the emcee announced. Candy grabbed my hand, just like I've seen beauty pageant contestants do on TV.

"The winner of the talent competition is"—he paused dramatically—"Helen Davis!" I gave a yelp and applauded madly. Helen and her escort walked up to the emcee, who handed her a rose and a plaque. Then they walked over to the side of the stage.

"Third runner-up—Donna Morelli!"

"Gee," whispered Candy to me as Donna went up to get her rose, "do you think she might have won if she hadn't dropped that egg?"

"Second runner-up—Patsy McCoy!"

"First runner-up—Marcia Jacobs!" My hands were stinging from clapping.

"And now, ladies and gentlemen, the moment you've all been waiting for—your new Miss Spring Valley—" There was a drumroll.

"Vicki Gilligan!"

Mechanically, I applauded along with everyone else. I wasn't surprised. She was beautiful, talented, and she had the "right" answer. As I watched Jeff escort her to the emcee to receive her crown, I honestly didn't feel the least bit jealous. I felt only relief that it was finally all over.

The scene in the auditorium was chaotic. Parents were hugging daughters, girlfriends were hugging boyfriends, and the candidates were hugging one another. There was a huge crowd around Vicki, and flashcubes kept popping as photographers took pictures of her and the runners-up.

"Honey, you were absolutely wonderful!" My mother threw her arms around me.

"You sure were," Dad said, pride written all over his face.

Dorie looked ecstatic. "Tina, you were fantastic!" Her eyes were wise, and she was gazing at me with something almost like adoration. I gave her a hug.

Then Ruth came running up, and there were more hugs. "I just saw Merrill, and she told me to tell you she's having a little celebration at her house."

165

"Great," I said, "I feel like a party. But I guess I'll have to ask Dave if he wants to go. After all, he *is* my escort." I looked around. "Where is he anyway?" He'd disappeared.

"I just saw him congratulating Vicki a minute ago," said Ruth.

"Have a good time at the party," Mom said. "You deserve it!"

I kissed my family goodbye and set off in search of Dave. He found me first. "Uh, Tina," he said uneasily, "I'm, well, I'm not feeling so great, you know? So look, I was wondering if maybe you could get a ride home with somebody—"

"Sure," I said, feeling nothing but relief at the thought of not having to spend the rest of the evening with him. "Thanks for escorting me, and I hope you feel better."

I knew he wasn't really sick. And five minutes later, when I saw him whispering with Vicki, I had a pretty good hunch as to whom he'd be leaving with. So where was Jeff?

As it turned out, he was right behind me. "Tina, I know you've probably heard this a hundred times tonight, but I have to say it, too. I'm so proud of you. What you did tonight took guts. That speech you gave, and your answer to the question—I was really impressed."

It was like a dream come true. He was saying everything I had wanted to hear him say. Well—almost everything. "Thanks, Jeff," I said.

"Where's Dave?" he asked.

"Not feeling well. I think he's leaving."

Jeff grinned. "Now isn't that a coincidence. Vicki's not feeling well either. Where does that leave us?"

I took a deep breath. "Together?"

Jeff leaned toward me, and right there in the middle of the auditorium he kissed me. "I love you, Tina," he whispered.

"Now I have everything," I murmured.

"What?"

I laughed. "Never mind. Let's go to the party."

"Sounds good to me," he replied. "I think we've got a lot to celebrate."

We hope you enjoyed reading this book. All the titles currently available in the Sweet Dreams series are listed on the next two pages. Ask for them in your local bookshop or newsagent. Two new titles are published each month.

If you would like to know more about Sweet Dreams, or if you have difficulty obtaining any of the books locally, or if you would like to tell us what you think of the series, write to:—

<u>United Kingdom</u>
Kim Prior,
Corgi Books,
Century House,
61-63 Uxbridge Road,
London W5 5SA,
England

<u>Australia</u>
Sally Porter,
Corgi and
Bantam Books,
26 Harley Crescent,
Condell Park 220,
N.S.W., Australia

17846 6	PORTRAIT OF LOVE (37)	Jeanette Nobile
17847 4	RUNNING MATES (38)	Jocelyn Saal
17848 2	FIRST LOVE (39)	Debra Spector
17849 0	SECRETS (40)	Anna Aaron
17850 4	THE TRUTH ABOUT ME AND BOBBY V (41)	Janetta Johns
17851 2	THE PERFECT MATCH (42)	Marian Woodruff
17850 2	TENDER LOVING CARE (43)	Anne Park
17853 9	LONG DISTANCE LOVE (44)	Jesse Dukore
17069 4	DREAM PROM (45)	Margaret Burman
17070 8	ON THIN ICE (46)	Jocelyn Saal
17071 6	TE AMO MEANS I LOVE YOU (47)	Deborah Kent
17072 4	DIAL L FOR LOVE (48)	Marian Woodruff
17073 2	TOO MUCH TO LOSE (49)	Suzanne Rand
17074 0	LIGHTS, CAMERA, LOVE (50)	Gailanne Maravel
17075 9	MAGIC MOMENTS (51)	Debra Spector
17076 7	LOVE NOTES (52)	Joanna Campbell
17087 2	GHOST OF A CHANCE (53)	Janet Quin-Harkin
17088 0	I CAN'T FORGET YOU (54)	Lois I. Fisher
17089 9	SPOTLIGHT ON LOVE (55)	Nancy Pines
17090 2	CAMPFIRE NIGHTS (56)	Dale Cowan
17871 9	ON HER OWN (57)	Suzanne Rand
17872 5	RHYTHM OF LOVE (58)	Stephanie Foster
17873 3	PLEASE SAY YES (59)	Alice Owen Crawford
17874 1	SUMMER BREEZES (60)	Susan Blake
17875 X	EXCHANGE OF HEARTS (61)	Janet Quin-Harkin
17876 8	JUST LIKE THE MOVIES (62)	Suzanne Rand
24150 8	KISS ME, CREEP (63)	Marian Woodruff
24151 6	LOVE IN THE FAST LANE (64)	Rosemary Vernon
24152 4	THE TWO OF US (65)	Janet Quin-Harkin
24153 2	LOVE TIMES TWO (66)	Stephanie Foster
24180 X	I BELIEVE IN YOU (67)	Barbara Conklin
24181 8	LOVEBIRDS (68)	Janet Quin-Harkin
24255 5	SPECIAL SOMEONE (70)	Terri Fields

NON-FICTION TITLES

17859 8	THE SWEET DREAMS BEAUTIFUL HAIR BOOK	Courtney DeWitt
17838 5	THE LOVE BOOK	Deidre Laiken and Alan Schneider
17845 8	THE BODY BOOK	Deidre Laiken and Alan Schneider
17077 5	HOW TO TALK TO BOYS AND OTHER IMPORTANT PEOPLE	Catherine Winters